Royal Time

Royal Time

RACHEL BRANTON

WHITE
STAR
PRESS

This is a work of fiction, and the views expressed herein are the sole responsibility of the author. Likewise, certain characters, places, and incidents are the product of the author's imagination, and any resemblance to actual persons, living or dead, or actual events or locales, is entirely coincidental.

Royal Time (Nobles of Beaumont, Book 4)

Published by White Star Press
P.O. Box 353
American Fork, Utah 84003

Printed in the United States of America
ISBN: 978-1-948982-37-5
Year of first printing: 2022

To my mother, who gave birth to and raised eight children. Her sacrifices taught me the importance of family and what really matters in life. (Hint: it's not a clean house.)

Chapter 1

Emerson

I stared at the sun-whitened stone of Castle Forêt's inner wall with a frown. Most of the stone making up the castle had held up well over the centuries, but this section had some serious issues.

"Sorry," I told my friend Harper Fontaine, whose recent marriage to the owner of the castle had provided me with the opportunity of a lifetime to re-engineer an ancient castle and the walls surrounding it. "This entire section will have to be removed completely and a new foundation set. The stones are unstable at best, which is why they've tilted or fallen. My guess is that when the king lived here in the late fourteenth century, they didn't only repurpose the stone in the outer wall to expand the main castle but also cannibalized these sections, and they were replaced later by someone who didn't really know what they were doing."

Harper sighed. "They were probably tired of hauling the

stones so far. Can't really blame them. And I doubt the king made it out this way very much."

"Well, at least the expansion on the castle itself was done correctly."

Because of this, we'd made excellent headway on the main castle since Harper's marriage five months earlier. But the walls around the courtyard were an issue she needed to make a decision on quickly for the renovations to continue on schedule.

"At least whoever replaced them did it with matching stones," came a disembodied voice from somewhere above us.

I squinted up into the late morning sun as my business partner and other best friend Amelia Giraud—or Mel for short—came into view on top of the wall. "Right," I agreed. "We can reuse most of these, so we won't have to bring in too much more stone."

"And we can fill in with stones still remaining in the outer wall." Mel carefully picked her way over the eroded stone to the tall ladder we'd brought for the purpose, her blond hair blowing in the early May breeze. "That's what we recommend. My calculations say there are enough to replace the damaged foundations and the stones suffering from the most erosion."

The past six months, we'd both put in long days, researching and studying the castle, our fresh engineering degrees from Stanford University not exactly up to the task of restoring ancient stone edifices. But we'd consulted with experts, hired several good local crews, and gained years of experience you couldn't get in a classroom. This wasn't a design on a computer in a high-rise office; we were in the trenches, and it was amazing.

A year ago last May, I had been the first to urge Mel to come to this country nestled between Switzerland and Germany near the French border to look for her half sister, Kami, who was married to Beaumont's king, but I'd never dreamed I'd stay—or that she and Harper would. Yet here they were married to native

Beaumontian nobles, and I would be here for at least another two years of renovation.

"Taking down the rest of the outer wall will change the land some," I added, "but using that stone is the best way to preserve history and keep the inner wall as close to the original as possible. But that only works if you're not going to replace the outer wall. If you're keeping it, we'll need more matching stone."

Harper, holding the ladder for Mel, waited until she was down to say, "Tristan and I have talked about that possibility, and we agree that replacing the outer wall is simply not feasible, even with his funds, except maybe the stair section that runs from the second courtyard down to the lake. What do you think about that?" Wind blew her dark hair into her mouth, and she swiped it away, turning her face to the breeze. "The records say the stairs were built at the same time as the castle enlargement when the king lived here. I'm not sure why they're not as well-engineered as the rest."

"I think that's a fantastic compromise," I told Harper. "And building next to the water is a lot more difficult than on dry land, so I'm not surprised sections there have the same issues. The walkway right off the courtyard is actually solid. I was thinking of using some of those stones to repair this wall because they're closer than the far outer wall, but if you want to keep the walkway to the stairs, we'll leave them. It'll be expensive to repair the stairs themselves but well worth it both in terms of resale value and use. Not that you're going to be selling the castle anytime soon." I grinned at her. "Too bad we can't go back in time to when the stones were first cannibalized so we could convince them to bring in new stone and engineer the lake stairs correctly. We'd have a lot less work to do now."

Harper laughed. "Right. Or to when they rebuilt the wall, so we could make them do the foundations better."

"Not sure I'd want to go back to either the fourteenth or sixteenth centuries," Mel put in with a little roll of her eyes. "Even here in Beaumont. Funny that the wall work they did two centuries after the castle expansion was so poorly done. You'd think they'd have learned more in that time. But even the walls built originally withstood better than the sixteenth-century repairs."

Harper grinned at us both. "I really appreciate your help on this. I know you've been putting in more than eight hours a day."

"Are you kidding? This is fun!" Mel hugged her.

Harper swirled her key ring around her finger. "Come on. I bet the guys are back with lunch." She and Mel started toward Harper's Jeep.

"Hey," I said. "Remember, I'm a guy too."

Mel snorted. "As if the constant stream of women you've been dating here didn't tell us that."

"I can't help it if these Beaumontian women love blond hair and killer green eyes." It was true. My looks were unusual among the sea of dark hair and eyes, and it made me stand out. Unfortunately, I hadn't yet found my soulmate like the girls had. It was enough to make me wonder if something was wrong with me. Recently, I'd even started turning down dating opportunities.

Mel must have noted something in my expression because she dropped back from Harper's side to walk with me. "Emerson Shaw, you are the most romantic man I know, including my husband, and you know how wonderful I think he is," she said, hooking her arm in mine and tilting her head to lay it briefly on my shoulder. "Of course women love you. Including us."

Everyone except one certain woman, I thought but refrained from saying as I opened the passenger front door for her and then climbed in the back seat, burying my hands in the pockets of my black leather jacket.

We drove over the dirt road until finally reaching the newly repaired cobbled drive that led up to the main castle. The castle had two beautiful turrets, hidden rooms, and even garderobes with ancient toilets that had once ingeniously dumped into an underground waterway leading down to the lake. Fortunately, those hadn't been used for at least a hundred years, and the analysis done on the lake showed that swimming was perfectly safe. One of the first things we'd done was to secure the turrets and plumb the bathrooms. The ballroom had been next since Harper and Tristan were nearly professional ballroom dancers, though neither would admit to it. Widening the entry doorway had been by far the biggest challenge, and I was still proud of the massive wood door we'd had specially constructed. It wasn't something a civil engineer would usually take care of, but I'd enjoyed it so much that I'd even helped the local artisan stain the door.

Harper and Mel's husbands, Tristan Fortier and Damien Giraud, were in the courtyard near the door to the modernized kitchen, which we'd moved from the courtyard itself to inside the castle proper. The men had positioned our meal on a stone table with matching stones that served as stools. Harper had moved several of the tables here from the countryside near the castle to the courtyard, where they would one day sit in the shade of some newly planted trees.

We walked under the archway leading into the courtyard, and the full table came into view. I stopped as I saw Jianne there— Lady Jianne Selmone, to be exact. My breath caught in my throat exactly as it had the moment I'd first seen her. My reaction had astounded me then—and still did. I had imagined myself in love before with other women, most recently Mel's young sister-in-law, who had ended up leaving Beaumont to study in England, but things felt different with Jianne from the very first day. My heart had somehow *known* her. That was what made this whole situation hard. Because she didn't seem to feel the same way or appear to even notice that I was serious about her. Despite my efforts to woo her, she never looked at me the way so many other women did, and I didn't know those women well enough to begin thinking seriously about them.

Oh, she laughed at my jokes and accepted my invitations to dinner, but she insisted on paying her half and introduced me to everyone as a friend. It bothered me. I even spent hours at her aunt's where she lived, listening to the older woman go on and on. Sure, the woman was an excellent cook, shooing away her servants so she could make exceptional meals for us in her enormous kitchen, but it was Jianne I really went there to spend time with. I think the old lady knew of my secret longing and approved, but that didn't make a difference to Jianne, and that worried me.

It also bothered me the way she sat so close to Tristan, who happened to be both a prince and a duke. She was his fourth cousin or something, and they'd dated shortly some time back, and while I knew he was completely in love with Harper now, maybe Jianne still felt something for him. Maybe that was why she wouldn't give me the time of day.

Romantically, that is.

But Jianne and Harper were good friends, and I should probably stop obsessing about how Jianne might feel about Tristan.

Mel and Harper rushed to greet their husbands with hugs and kisses, and I felt a tug of jealousy. Mel and I'd once had an understanding that if we both weren't married by a certain age, we'd marry each other and raise a couple of kids, which we both wanted. While I was happy for her, and in no way pining for lost chances, her good fortune—and Harper's—only made my current lifestyle unsatisfying. Although maybe it wasn't their relationships that had made the difference but meeting Jianne. Before she entered my life, I hadn't worried about the future.

Now I had the strange sensation of being the only one looking in from the outside.

"Hey, Jianne," I said, coming to her side. "Nice to see you. I didn't realize you'd be here."

She smiled, and my heart did a funny little wonderful dance that almost felt painful. "Harper wanted my help with the dining and guest rooms," she said in very good British English, "so I decided to take a couple days off from my current project and make it a long weekend. I have some ideas about how we can remodel the old kitchen in the second courtyard into an outside barbeque for entertaining purposes. It would be the perfect backdrop for a swimming pool."

I settled on the stone stool next to hers. "That's a great idea. There's plenty of space now that they don't need to house soldiers, though you gotta admit, having an authentic medieval garrison here would be awesome."

She laughed. "It would, yes, but only if they were in proper uniform. My aunt has an entire collection of clothing from that period that's been handed down through the generations. I bet some of those were worn at this very castle."

"We should hold a medieval ball here after we complete the castle renovations. Maybe she'd lend us a few costumes."

Her eyebrows raised together in that way I loved. I'd tried teaching her to arch just one, but she was one of the few people in the world who couldn't do it. We'd spent countless hours trying and laughing.

"A ball?" she challenged. "I thought you hated those things."

Not when I'm with you, I wanted to say, but that was too forward for where our relationship was.

"It's possible, I suppose, that she might lend the reproductions she has made but never the originals," she went on without seeming to expect an answer. "Those are way too brittle. She's extremely protective of even the reproductions, but she likes you. They are currently in France on a temporary display, or she would have shown them to you, I'm sure."

"She did mention them once or twice." My head had been full of Jianne, but I wasn't that inattentive. I actually liked the old woman.

"You are always sweet with her." Jianne touched my bare forearm, and it took a concentrated effort not to put my hand over hers and bring it to my lips.

"So what about the stables?" I asked to distract myself. "Keep them or take them out?"

"Out," Harper said, sitting on the tall stone next to Jianne, where Tristan had been when we'd come into the courtyard. "You know that old entry I told you I wanted to make wider? That will lead to the new stables outside the walls. Much better pasture for them when we're here, and much less smell."

Jianne laughed again, and my eyes found their way back to her. She had the most beautiful wavy dark hair and brown eyes so deep they pulled me in. Three tiny freckles nestled in an arc under her right eye near her nose, and there were two more on the other side. I loved those freckles with a passion that was probably unhealthy. Harper once said that Jianne had the kind of looks that men went to war for, and I had to agree. She'd been sitting at least a foot away from Tristan when we arrived, and I'd wanted to punch his face.

"Well, I'm glad you're here," I told Jianne. "I'd like to get your opinion on the stairs down to the lake while you're here this weekend." She always had good suggestions, even on the engineering side of things. She had a way of making everything she touched more beautiful.

"Yes," Harper agreed, "I'd love your opinion." She stared at me hard behind Jianne's head in some warning that escaped me altogether.

I ignored her. Jianne was perfectly able to take care of herself. The one time two weeks ago when I'd almost kissed her at her aunt's, she'd laughed in my face. I hadn't dared try again. Yet.

Mel pushed a couple of wrapped sandwiches in our direction. Her eyes were laughing, and I suspected she knew my thoughts. Mel knew far too much about me. My life would have been so much easier if we'd fallen in love, but the occasional kisses we'd shared over the years with that hope in mind had fallen dismally flat for both of us.

"Thanks." Jianne swept up a sandwich. "I love these."

"It's just a sandwich," I said.

"No, it's a jambon de forêt sandwich made by Viviana Bazin," Tristan corrected as he sat down next to his wife. "They can trace their ancestors back to the fourteenth century. Apparently when the royal family lived here at the castle, their family was highly favored by the queen."

I began to unwrap the fat little bundle. "Oh, now I remember you talking about these." The sandwiches were made of some kind of special ham with killer bread baked by a local woman at a tiny dive of a restaurant called The Chef's Table. But a sandwich was a sandwich, after all, so I was prepared to be underwhelmed. At least they'd also bought pastries.

"He's not kidding," Damien said as if sensing my skepticism. "They're so good that I'm tempted to buy the restaurant."

Tristan smirked. "Already tried. No deal."

I studied the sandwich momentarily. There were layers of ham and lettuce and tomatoes. Nothing overtly special. The aroma of the bread, though, was heady. I bit into it—then again and again before I slowed down enough to admit that it was the best sandwich I'd ever eaten.

"Ah-ha." Jianne grinned at me. "You like it?"

"It's okay," I conceded. "Actually, I'm thinking about asking this Viviana out. Maybe she'd give me the recipe for the bread."

Jianne laughed with abandon, head back, her white throat exposed. It looked so soft that I wanted to . . .

I nearly choked as she bumped my arm with hers and sent an electrical shock racing up my skin. "You're so funny," she said. "But I bet she has a daughter or granddaughter you could date."

"I won't settle," I insisted. *For anyone but you.* I hurriedly took another bite to distract myself from those dangerous thoughts.

"So give us the rundown," Tristan said after swallowing his own mouthful. "Harper texted that the foundations in the wall aren't great. Is that going to add time?"

"Actually, we think we can hit or beat our current two-year goal if we use the existing stone from the outer wall," Mel began, launching into details of the build. I was content to let her do the talking while I concentrated on my amazing sandwich. She summed up her spiel with, "We'll update the engineering plan, but basically, it means big equipment and manpower."

I downed the last bit of my sandwich with a drink of Beaumontian soda that tasted like Dr. Pepper with a hint of lime. "The trickiest part will still be stabilizing the ramparts near the back part of the castle and either adding a wall or a railing. I'm assuming you don't want your kids taking nosedives from the walk. They didn't seem to care that much back in the old days. Guess soldiers were expendable."

"Or just sure-footed," Tristan quipped. "Especially our soldiers." That had Jianne laughing again. It was a beautiful sound, even if her attention was on him.

I set my drink down and stood. "I'm going to walk down to the lake. I'd like to get a jumpstart on seeing what's there now that I know Harper wants to keep it. Save me some of those pastries."

"No guarantees," Tristan said.

Everyone laughed except Mel, who was watching me, a worried line between her eyes. "I'd better go too," she said. "Can't have him getting the credit for all the good ideas. I'll bring my phone and double-check the measurements I already took of the stairs on my engineering app." Of course, she was actually coming to grill me about my feelings. Sometimes having two women as your best friends was annoying. I'd have to make a point to spend more time with their husbands.

"That useless thing?" I teased. "Phone apps have no business in real engineering."

"Ha!" Mel said. "You'll see. It will save our bacon one day."

"Only if my computer dies and the internet goes out permanently." It was an argument we enjoyed repeating.

"Well, I'm going too." Jianne stepped off her stool. "To make sure these two don't drown each other over an app. Besides, I've never actually been down to the lake, and since Harper and Emerson asked me for advice, I want to make sure there's a nice place for a gazebo on the dock."

"Great idea." I was suddenly feeling happier than I had moments before, though technically I'd been trying to get some distance between myself and everyone—especially Jianne. Although since I had asked her opinion, maybe a part of me had not-so-secretly hoped she'd come along.

"You guys go without us," Harper said. "Tristan and Damien promised to help me with the shades in the ballroom. The installers didn't get them right, but they are too high for me to fix by myself. It shouldn't take long. We'll come down after."

Mel grabbed the box of pastries. "Just to make sure you do, I'll take these with us for safekeeping. If you want them, you'll have to join us. You guys bring the drinks."

Harper grinned her acceptance of the terms, so Jianne, Mel,

and I went through to the second courtyard and out the back entrance. The women chattered as we crossed the field to where the walkway from the ramparts led off the outer courtyard and fell into ruins as it angled down toward the water. I was content to let their voices play over me, noting that this land had likely looked very similar for hundreds of years. How many peasants and nobles had walked this very path?

"There should be a large patio here at the summit," Jianne said as we reached the first ruins of the stairs. She walked ahead of us between the scattered stones and wildflowers, her hands outstretched as if getting a feel for the place. A breeze stirred the end of her red-patterned dress and the coils of her long, dark hair. "Look. The stairs have prevented the tree growth here, so we have a marvelous view all the way down to the water."

For a moment, I couldn't breathe, seeing her there, her arms stretched out. The idea of staying here and working closely with her for two more years was both a delicious promise and a terrifying sentence, depending on her feelings for me.

"Give her time," Mel said softly from beside me.

I jerked my head toward her, having forgotten she was there. "What do you mean?" My voice was thick with disuse or maybe emotion.

"I don't know all the details," she said softly, "but I gather from Harper that Jianne had a hard life growing up with her father. Haven't you ever wondered why she lives with her aunt and not with him? Or on her own?"

"I guess I thought it was a chaperone kind of thing that nobility do in Beaumont."

She laughed. "Maybe a little. But for her there's another reason."

I knew more than I was letting on, of course, about Jianne's controlling jerk of a father, but I wondered if maybe there was something else that had something to do with why Jianne and Tristan had only dated for a few months. "Anyway, Jianne treats me like a brother. Like you do."

Mel shrugged. "It's not like us, but maybe that's what she needs right now."

"Great."

Mel's smirk widened at the frustration in my voice. "Think of it as justice. It's about time you know how all those women who fall in love with you feel." Before I could answer, she hurried forward to join Jianne, who had stopped to pick a bright purple wildflower.

We examined the wall of the walkway where it met the crumbling stairs, with Mel taking notes on her phone. Afterward, we made our way down into the small valley among the grass and shrubs, examining the stones of the staircase itself.

"Not as bad as I thought," I said as we approached the water. "Though some definite structural problems. You know, I think there might have been a flood or something here that added to the issues."

Mel trailed her fingers along the white stone. "Could be."

"Look!" Jianne said, pointing. "A little door."

Sure enough, a short, heavily worn wooden door had been set into the side wall of the staircase. "Must be storage for gardening tools," I said. "Looks to be well above the current water level. But it could be access to a plumbing exit leading down from the castle kitchens or something."

"Let's open it and see." Jianne grinned at me temptingly.

How could I say no?

The wood of the door was swollen, but it wasn't locked, and with the aid of a stick and a bit of brute force, I was able to get it open. Ducking my head and using my phone as a flashlight, I peered inside. "Looks like an actual hallway. Some kind of stone on the floor." I pushed against the walls before bending and going inside.

Jianne crowded in after me. "Short gardeners," she whispered.

"And skinny ones," I said. "It looks a little wider up there." Six more feet and I stepped into a small room with a waist-high circular stone structure. "Looks like a well."

"Not a well," Mel said, balancing her box of pastries on the circular stone wall and peering inside. "Looks like access to a passageway for water waste." She pointed to a large hole several feet down. "Might be what's connected to that hole we found in the kitchen. I bet it's a tunnel from there, just like there were tunnels from the garderobes' towers."

Jianne drew a swift breath of air and pushed past me to where a small wooden bucket sat on a stone ledge set into the wall. Inside the bucket, various tools looked as if they had just been stored by their owner. She dug through them. "A billhook and a hammer. And look at this saw. From the seventeenth century, if not from much earlier. We have to take these to Tristan and Harper. At the very least, they'll want to display them at the castle."

I examined the tools, which appeared slightly rusted but in rather good shape for being hidden here this long. "They really are something."

From the room, a narrow corridor angled to the left as if continuing into the side of the hill. "I wonder what else is in here?" I mused.

"We've come far enough," Mel warned, picking up the box of pastries. "We'll need to get safety gear at the very least. And test the stones as we go."

"Let's hurry and get what we need then." Jianne picked up the bucket of tools. "I want to change into pants." She grinned at me with excitement that matched my own.

I winked at her, though she probably didn't see it in the dim light. "Let's do it."

We pushed through the tiny corridor until we were once again outside, blinking at the brightness of the afternoon sun.

Mel and Jianne turned toward the bottom of the staircase, probably intending to examine the stairs there before starting up the other side, but I didn't follow. "Wait a minute," I said. "Something's not right."

"What do you mean?" Jianne paused and looked back at me, a smudge of dust on her face that I really wanted to brush away—any excuse to touch her.

Focus, I told myself.

"Those stairs didn't look like that when we got here." I felt a little crazy saying it, but the stairway had been falling apart, and now only the bottom section was constructed—and less than halfway at that. The ceiling of the room we'd just left wasn't finished, and there was no door, ancient or otherwise.

Mel gasped. "He's right. What happened to the staircase?"

"And look at the lake!" Jianne's face creased in worry. "The trees are different, and the water isn't clear anymore. It's . . . polluted. Are those dead fish?"

"Never mind the fish," Mel said. "Let's get up there and see what's happened." She motioned to the top of the valley.

We hurried up the slope until we reached the top where we'd stood only thirty minutes before among a litter of fallen stones. It was the same little valley with the same natural lake, and we could see the castle in the distance, but everything else was completely changed.

Jianne

The stairway had only a few sections that were under construction, and those began near the lake in the area we'd just left. There were no stones angling up the valley, and with the way the grass was growing on several of the huge boulders, the construction near the lake looked as if it had halted some months earlier at the beginning of spring, or perhaps before the first snowfall the previous October or November.

In silence, we turned again to look at the castle in the distance, beyond the large fields now stretching out before us, the neatly planted rows dotted with people dressed in medieval peasant garb.

"Where are we?" Mel asked. "This doesn't make sense. And are those peasants over there?"

I experienced dizziness as the blood seemed to flee my body. "This may sound crazy, but I think the better question might be *when* are we."

Before Emerson and Mel could respond to my crazy sugges-
tion, a wizened man dressed in a dirty tunic and even dirtier
leggings came toward us, waving his hands and yelling in a loud
voice as he pointed at the wooden bucket of tools.

"What's he saying?" Mel whispered. "I thought I was getting
pretty good at understanding French."

"It's an older version," I said. "I learned some of the differences
because of my aunt, but at any rate, I do seem to understand what
he's saying. He wants his tools."

"His tools? Oh!" Emerson pushed the bucket at the old man.
"Pardonnez-moi," he said.

The old man wrapped his long arm around the bucket and
glared at Emerson, his face flushing, and then he was off again,
speaking rapidly and waving his other arm like a lunatic. At one
point, he gestured to Emerson's clothing, then Mel's, and finally
darted a glance at my red dress, which, compared to the women
in the field behind him, had a lot less material than what might be
considered modest for the era, though not enough for his face to
flush the way it did. Maybe he was still angry.

When the tirade ended, he turned to a mud-streaked boy and
flung a couple of sentences at him like a blow. With a frightened
glance at us, the child took off running.

"Did he just say something about guards?" Emerson asked.
"Because as weird as it might seem, I think I'm starting to understand him."

I nodded, unable to speak through my growing dread. Neither
of us should have been able to understand much of those rapid
words.

"This has got to be some kind of a joke," Mel said, staring
around us. "But how could Harper have pulled it off? We haven't
been out here that long." She squinted down at the lake. "Do you
think it's some kind of holograph?"

"We don't have that technology yet," Emerson said. "Not outside like this. And the only other explanation is aliens or . . ."

"Time travel," I finished, starting back down the valley. "We have to get back."

"What?" Emerson sounded surprised. "If it really is time travel, I'd think you'd be anxious to explore while we're here."

"No." I stopped and faced them. "People died all the time back in the Middle Ages, which is what this has to be since those stairs aren't finished. The king was actually murdered in the four-teenth century shortly after the renovations on this castle were completed."

Emerson blinked. "He was murdered here?"

"No. After he left for the palace, and I don't know much about that, but there was an attempt on his life here first. No one was ever charged with it. His brother became king regent until the king's only son came of age."

"And you're worried they'll try to pin the murder attempt on us?" he asked.

I frowned. "Well, you're not exactly a background type of person, Emerson, are you?"

"I didn't think you noticed." His grin did something to my heart, which I had studiously tried to ignore ever since I met him eight months ago when Harper and Tristian first introduced us. The last thing I wanted was to need him. I couldn't fall back into the old ways of allowing any man to eat at my self-esteem and make me question everything I did. Not that it was Emerson I didn't trust. It was me and how long I'd allowed myself to remain under my father's controlling thumb. For the first time in my life, I was someone of value, and I wanted to keep it that way.

I rolled my eyes. "Come on, let's go see if we can reverse what-ever this is."

"It can't be time travel," Mel said, her voice strained. She looked pale, and her fingers were gripping the pastry box so tightly that the sweets inside were in serious jeopardy. "That's impossible."

"I guess." I took longer steps, though my flat pumps weren't exactly good for speed on this hill.

Emerson caught up to me with a couple steps of his long legs. "What do you mean, I guess?"

I glanced over at him. "There were rumors."

"What rumors?"

I shook my head. "Just some stuff my aunt uncovered in her research of period clothing. A few pieces she found appeared to be authentic but in pristine condition. She was told by the woman she purchased them from that her grandmother claimed to have brought them back after a time travel episode. No one believed her, of course, but there were the clothes as proof. I examined them myself several times. They were perfectly authentic."

Emerson stared at me as if I'd lost my mind. I felt something recoil inside me, and I tripped on a rock, twisting my ankle. Emerson grabbed me before I fell. "Easy," he said.

"You think I'm crazy." My surge of resentment was out of proportion to his reaction, but the emotion was a defensive mechanism that had kicked in since taking control of my life. Some days it was a constant battle to remind myself that not everyone wanted to offend or hurt me.

"For going down this hill at that speed in those shoes?" He grinned. "Yes. But not about the clothes. I still keep thinking it's some kind of elaborate prank, but I believe you about the clothes." He shrugged. "It would be fantastic if it could all be true." He looked around eagerly, but his smile soon faded. "Except for the, you know, dying part."

I couldn't help grinning back at him. Every time I thought he'd mock me, he never did. Not about the important things. But that didn't mean anything, did it?

I became aware of his eyes on my lips and realized he was still holding me. My heart gave an excited *thump!* despite my lack of permission. I pulled away, gingerly putting weight on my ankle.

"You okay?" he asked.

I nodded. "Just a bit sore. You caught me before I came down too hard. Thanks."

"Anytime."

Mel pushed past us. "Let's hurry. I don't like any of this."

"And here I thought you'd be eager to study more ancient architecture," Emerson teased, but when Mel turned a horrified stare in his direction, he sobered. "What is it, Mel?"

"Nothing." But there was something—we could both feel it. "Let's just go back inside to where that circle of stone was," she added. "Maybe we'll find answers."

But at the base of the hill there were no answers because in the half-finished little room the circle of stone didn't exist. Only a deep hole that no one wanted to climb down. We walked around the entire structure, staying close to one another, but nothing happened.

When we finally gave up, Emerson contemplated a nearby pile of square-cut stones, his strong arms folded across his abdomen. "Maybe we need to build it," he said. "So weird that this would happen when we were just joking about having the chance to go back in time to build it right the first time."

"You were?" I asked.

Mel nodded. "We were."

Somehow it was all connected. But if we had gone back in time to the fourteenth century, where family and connections were everything, the three of us would have nothing. My mind raced, trying to remember what I knew about my own family, or maybe Tristan's since we were distantly related. The castle had been a present to Tristan's third great-grandfather on his mother's side

when he was given the title Duc de Vallée for being a loyal knight
and leader of the king's army—the king at the time happened to be
his eighth great-grandfather on his father's side, and mine as well
because we shared a second great grandfather in that line. So while
Tristan's ancestors on his father's side had built the castle, ownership
had come down to him through his mother's family line. But all of
this happened long after the fourteenth century. I needed to think
further up the line. Was the name Selmone in use earlier? Our original holdings were in northern Beaumont. I knew that much.

Voices came to us from the top of the valley, and dread filled my
stomach as I recognized the tunics and armor of the king's guard,
four of them, who were apparently in a great hurry to reach us.

"Oh, no," I said.

Emerson stepped in front of me, gesturing for Mel to get
behind him in one of his magnanimous gestures. He had no way
of knowing that men were plentiful in Beaumont during this era
while women, at least women of gentry, were few and far between.
If the king or one of his court nobles had an interest in us, Emerson
was as good as buried if he tried to defend us.

I tugged on his shirt. "Let me," I said, gathering my courage.
"Your accent is atrocious. Please."

He contemplated me for the time it took the guards to hurtle
halfway down the hill. "Okay," he said finally, "But if they so
much as lay a hand on you—"

"They won't. But you have to do as I say." I glanced back at
the stones, hoping they would magically reappear and form that
little room.

They didn't.

The soldiers came to a halt a spear's length from us, which was
easy to see since they carried both spears and swords. The little boy
and the old man were with them.

"Who are you?" a guard demanded in ancient French, though

my mind simplified the actual words. "What unnatural garb is this you wear? Are you a witch?"

"Nay, not a witch," I said. "I am Lady Jianne Selmone, a distant cousin of the king. I have come with my sister, Amelia, and my brother, Emerson, to see the marvelous castle we have heard so much about even where we live in northern Beaumont."

The guard's eyes narrowed. "The gardener accuses you of absconding with his tools."

"Nay, my good man. We found them abandoned and restored them to him. As you can see, he has possession of them now."

"Hmm. Northern Beaumont. We shall see." The words sounded like a threat. "Come, we'll take you to the king and his brother to see if you are who you say you are." He gestured to the other three guards to surround us.

His mention of the king verified my guess about the time period because as far as I knew, the only time the king had lived in Forêt for an extended period was during the fourteenth century reconstruction.

"Pray tell," I said. "What happened to halt the construction here? Is there not supposed to be a staircase that joins with the walkway along the castle wall? We heard it was so."

"Aye," the guard said reluctantly, casting his dark gaze at the abandoned stone. "The master mason fell ill on his journey to inspect and bring new stone, and the king is reluctant to move forward without his guidance."

"Then we may be of some help," Emerson said. "We know about masonry."

The guard's eyes fell over us. "All of you?"

I cast Emerson a hard look. Now was not the time to be spouting praises for Mel's engineering prowess. "My brother is a skilled engineer," I explained. "We simply enjoy hearing his discourse. He is quite revered in the north."

"I thought engineers designed catapults and other war machines," the guard said, his voice slightly less terse now.

"Perhaps. But my brother's expertise is to design structures."

"Well, we have many masons under the master mason."

"I am sure it is so." Likely their master mason had advanced training in engineering and architecture, even if the guards didn't understand that.

"Come." He gestured for us to follow him.

"Brother?" Emerson stepped close to say in English as we began trudging back up the hill. "I mean, Mel and I can pass with our blond hair, but you and I don't look much alike. Wouldn't it be safer if I weren't your brother?"

"Only if you want to risk being killed so that some noble can court one of us," I told him, my voice barely audible over our footsteps. "Being a brother is much safer in this era. It means you have charge of us, but you aren't in the way of a beneficial match. The king will have many nobles hanging around him wherever he goes, even here in the country."

His brow crinkled. "Well, you are beautiful, so I guess that makes sense." He didn't sound happy about it, though.

I tried not to let his comment about my looks go to my head. I knew I was attractive. Even my abusively controlling father had pointed that out—but then in the same breath he'd . . .

No, what he'd said didn't matter. I knew who I was now. I was smart and strong and capable. And kind. Those were the adjectives that were important to me. I just had to keep reminding myself until I believed it in my core. Equally important was surrounding myself with people who encouraged me to choose my own path.

Which wasn't exactly allowed for women in the fourteen hundreds.

"I don't like this," Mel whispered from behind me. "This isn't a prank, is it?"

I shook my head. "No, definitely not. Those tunics and swords are authentic. I'd stake my life on that."

Her face was even paler than before. "Then how are we going to get home? Am I ever going to see Damien again?"

"We'll figure something out." Emerson put his arm around Mel, taking the box of pastries from her. I was glad he could give her comfort because I was too numb to reach out. I had to figure out what to do next so we wouldn't all end up in some unmarked grave.

Chapter 3

Emerson

Her brother. Of all the ways for her to introduce me, I hadn't expected that. It made sense with her explanation, but quite frankly, I'd rather pose as her husband or fiancé than let any noble think she was fair game. How could I protect her from that if I was only her brother?

Jianne's face was pale, but she looked determined, and her story about her family had been quick thinking on her part. I only hoped it had some root in reality and that the lack of transportation and communication in this era would keep our guise intact until we could find a way home.

Mel wasn't holding up nearly as well, which was surprising given her independent nature. She leaned into me heavily, looking broken, as if the idea of being separated from Damien was more than she could take, and I could understand that, but we'd muddle through together the way we always had until we could reunite them.

We reached the top of the valley, and once again, the white stone of the castle came into view under the afternoon sun. We began our way through the fields. Everything was familiar but in an odd way. The vegetation was different, but the castle walls themselves were largely unchanged with time. The castle court-yard bustled with activity, especially in the outdoor kitchen. There were animals prowling and people working and laughing, all of them wrinkled from prolonged exposure to the sun. Their clothes weren't clean, and some were missing teeth and even limbs, and occasionally the body odor had me gagging.

This was definitely not the twenty-first century. I hadn't really worried about the actuality of time travel until now when it hit us in the face—or rather, in the olfactory senses.

People parted as our guard shouted for them to get out of the way. He shoved a few people who were too slow and kicked a dog-sized pig, who was probably going to be the king's supper. Peasants, soldiers, and tradesmen alike stared at us as if we were some kind of novelty. Ripples of whispered conversation waved around the courtyard, just beyond understanding, though I caught the word *dress* and *witch*. Not a good sign.

Mel had regained strength and was walking on her own now, but I didn't like her paleness. It wasn't like her. Had she come down with some strange medieval disease? No, I was pretty sure we hadn't been here long enough for that.

Jianne held herself erect, like the lady she was, and my admi-ration for her increased. She was frightened, like all of us, but she was also resolute and determined. She glanced in my direction, and I gave her an encouraging grin, arching one brow as a subtle reminder of our game together.

She laughed aloud, causing the guard to pause. "Something amuses you, Lady Selmone?"

"It is naught. Pray do not concern yourself," she said, with a royal haughtiness that immediately put him in his place.

We were taken into a side entrance which I would enlarge in the future, and as we went through the castle, I noted that all the renovations that had been completed in the fourteenth century were largely completed. Which made sense as the builder would have completed the castle first before the stairs to the lake. Only the front portion of the castle, which would someday become the ballroom, was unfinished and boarded up as it awaited the return of the builder.

The guards led us to a reception chamber, which would one day be the sitting room, and the king arrived shortly with a thin, bookish man in tow. King Lacort was shorter than I expected and stocky, but he had the same dark hair and eyes that marked most of his country's population. He wore no hat, and his snug pants and rich blue tunic were surprisingly conservative.

"His Majesty Bérenger Louis Lacort," the thin man said with a flourish of his slender hand. He waved the guards to the back wall, then adjusted his black, flat-topped hat, which appeared in danger of falling off his head.

"Lady Selmone," the king said with a jovial smile on his rounded face. "I know of your family, but I am afraid I do not remember your name."

Jianne curtseyed grandly as if she'd been doing so all her life, which I guess she had since she was related to royalty. "Jianne," she said. "And this is my sister, Amelia, whom we affectionately call Mel, and our brother, Emerson." Mel tried to copy her curtsey to less successful results, and I merely bowed, which was a lot easier. "We are pleased to see Your Highness," Jianne added. "We apologize for not sending word of our arrival."

He took her hand and kissed it, but not lingeringly, so I kept my peace—especially after Jianne shot a warning glance in my direction. "It is us who are pleased that you have chosen to journey south," King Lacort said. "You are on your way to the capital city, I presume? At any rate, I am pleased by your visit, and my wife will be too. She has a dire need of company here as she has banished most of her ladies and my noblemen because of the current construction."

"The pleasure of her company will be all ours," Jianne responded.

King Lacort motioned to the thin man. "This is Fredrick, my friend and castle steward. If you need anything during your stay, please consult with him, and he will arrange it."

"Thank you, Sire." Jianne curtseyed again.

"I believe I have not had the fortune to be with your parents since they came for my coronation," the king continued. "If I remember correctly, you and your sister were only babies." His eyes brushed mine. "I don't recall meeting you, however, Lord Selmone."

I was startled to be called by Jianne's last name, and I bit my tongue so I wouldn't correct him. Not exactly the way I'd seen the future going. Or, in this case, the past.

"He had to stay home and take care of our father's holdings," Jianne said without hesitation, which was kind of amusing since I was the same age as Mel, and Jianne was only a year younger than us.

"Indeed. You are all welcome here. But what's this the guard tells me of Lord Selmone's abilities with masonry? Is it true?" The words were addressed to Jianne, but he was looking at me. She bit her bottom lip as she widened her eyes at me, indicating that I should answer.

"Yes, Your Majesty," I said. "My specialty is building by the water. If it pleases you, I could look at the construction by the lake." I butchered the French badly, and trying to add in the pretty phrase "if it pleases you" made it worse. The king looked in confusion at Jianne.

"You will have to excuse our brother," she said. "He was largely educated in Rome and hence lacking the finer skills of communicating properly in French. But he is a wonder with stone, especially for structures built near water, and he is happy to be of use to you, if you so desire. We heard that your master mason fell ill." She dipped her head in Mel's direction. "My sister often serves as my brother's secretary, so she is versed in masonry as well."

"Does she now?" The king's eyes landed on Mel. "Oh, but she looks quite unwell."

"Indeed," Jianne said. "It has been an arduous journey."

"Ah, yes." The king looked over in relief as a woman swept into the room, followed by a butler in a stiff, formal tunic. "Here is my lady queen now. She will be happy to see you settled."

"Her Highness, Sophia Elisabeth Lacort," the butler intoned, with a little bow in the queen's direction.

The queen was a round, large-busted woman with a kind face that was handsome rather than beautiful beneath an overpowering layer of rouge. She was at least ten years younger than her husband, perhaps thirty, and her hair was almost as light as Mel's. "Welcome," she said with a serene smile. "I am so glad to greet relatives of my husband." She leaned forward and crushed first Jianne and then Mel to her chest before offering her hand to me, which I bowed over, offering her a smile that I hoped struck the right note between friendship and respect. I didn't want to end up with my head on the chopping block if the king turned out to be a jealous man.

"May we have your chests brought up?" the queen asked.

"I fear our belongings have been delayed," Jianne said.

"Never mind," the queen said, waving the words aside with a plump hand. "Do not trouble yourself over that inconvenience.

Several of my ladies are your size, and we will find you both something suitable to wear." She eyed Mel's jeans and added, "I've always wanted to wear a man's trousers, but I'm afraid my husband isn't quite so modern."

The king laughed. "No, indeed. I like my women to look like women." He raised a finger. "I mean my woman," he said with another hearty laugh as he leaned over to kiss his wife. They shared a glance that I recognized only too well, having seen it on the faces of my two best friends and their new husbands. Whatever else the king might be, he loved his wife, and that made me relax. Maybe I didn't need to be Jianne's pretend brother after all.

"Come along," said the queen, with a tiny, elegant wave at Jianne and Mel. I had to wonder if such a gesture was inherited or learned.

I took a step after them but stopped awkwardly as I realized I was not included in their little party. Mel looked back at me, grabbed the box of pastries, and mouthed, "Behave," but Jianne didn't look back as she left, and I wondered what that might mean.

King Lacort stepped in my direction, looking up at me to say, "I would love to hear your ideas regarding the stairway to the lake as that has been a particular concern for my master mason. Master Garnier is a skilled architect and engineer, and, in fact, he built the exquisite monastery in the south of Beaumont, if you have ever had the occasion to see it."

"I have, actually. It's magnificent. He is indeed skilled." Even after centuries, the multi-turreted edifice was an architectural and engineering marvel. No wonder the renovations on the castle had lasted so long.

The king's grin spread. "I am pleased you agree. However, the work came to a stop several months ago when he fell ill. The masons and carpenters under him have continued the work here at the castle according to his plan, but there was a disagreement about the staircase, so it has not continued. There has also been a lack of communication with the quarry for the stone. Anyway, I expect him back shortly, but he says building by the lake will be difficult."

"The main difference with building by water is the foundation," I said. "It has to be deeper and stronger, and we'll need, uh, metal rods . . . you have a blacksmith here, right?"

"Indeed, I have one of the best. Come, let's go down to the lake."

"Now?" I asked in surprise.

The king looked at the butler, who was still hovering nearby. "Have them bring around the horses."

"Yes, Sire." He bowed before disappearing into the hall.

The steward glanced at me before saying, "Should we arrange attire for Lord Selmone before our ride?"

Though the king had previously called me Lord Selmone, it took me a moment to remember that I was that lord. *Okay then.* I shook my head.

"Nay," the king said, noting my expression. "My cousin and I are eager to be off." My estimation of him continued to rise.

Within a few minutes, I found myself on horseback with the king, his steward, and four guards. I was grateful for the fact that as I'd lived among nobles the past year, my riding skills had greatly improved, though this medieval saddle was definitely more challenging to use—and far more uncomfortable.

Down at the lake, I studied the structure, though from well outside the partially finished room. As much as I wanted to return to my own time, I wouldn't leave Jianne and Mel to face the mercy of the Middle Ages alone. Finally, I asked for a shovel and began digging up a goodly amount of dirt to see what the foundation looked like. It took a long time to dig a trench, but after a while the king made the guards take a turn. We were shoulder deep and twice the length of a grave before I was satisfied that we'd uncovered enough to quadruple-check my suspicions. I squatted inside the ditch to examine the stones, and sure enough, while the foundation was better than it needed to be on solid ground, this close to the lake where the moisture content in the soil was high, all it needed was one really wet year to cause failure.

I climbed from the ditch to explain my findings to the king. "It's good the construction was halted," I said, trying to think of fancy words I might have heard in medieval shows to convey my point. "My fears are confirmed. As it is now, this structure cannot withstand a moderately wet year without significant failure."

"Preposterous," said a voice behind me.

I turned in surprise because the voice sounded like the king, yet not quite. Staring at me was a man who was a good three inches taller than King Lacort, nearly approaching my own six feet two inches. He had the same coloring, stocky build, and round face as the king, but his hair was longer, his pants ballooned wider around his buttocks, and his purple patterned tunic was far more pompous. The elaborate hat on his head was a monstrosity. Clearly, he had to be a close relative, one with an over-inflated ego or absolutely no fashion sense. Though for all I knew, maybe it was the king whose outfit was too conservative for his importance.

"Ah, brother," the king said, "this is our distant cousin, Lord Selmone." To me, he added, "Lord Selmone, I present my brother, Constantine Jehan Lacort, Duc de la Rivière Cristal."

Which I was pretty sure meant Duke of the Crystal River, which was a sizable valley in southeastern Beaumont. I nodded. "Nice—uh, pleasure to meet you, Duc Lacort."

"I'm sure," Constantine said without extending his hand. "So you're a cousin, are you? Why do you think you know better than our craftsmen?"

"Easy, Constantine." The king placed a hand on his brother's arm. "Lord Selmone is a trained architect. I requested that he give us his expert opinion."

Constantine's chin lifted slightly. "There is no need for more opinions. I have arranged stone, and I have spoken with Master Garnier. He has agreed that the work will continue until he returns."

"Excellent," the king said, placing a hand on his brother's arm. I thought that would be the end of it, but the king continued, "Even so, I'd like to hear what Lord Selmone has to say." He gestured for me to continue my explanation.

Constantine's mouth twisted, but he didn't say anything. Instead, he stepped closer to the ditch and stared down at the uncovered foundation stones.

I tried to think up more phrases that sounded medieval, failing miserably, but at least I understood eighty percent of what they were saying, which was good for me. "For most years," I said, "the footings here are adequate. However, there are always years when we receive more rains, flooding even."

"That is true." The king looked over the lake. "I remember hearing about flooding all over Beaumont as a boy."

"Yes, but we are ending the stairs significantly before the bank," Constantine said. "The waters have never reached that far."

"Not at any mark we can see," I said. "However, the earth underneath also becomes saturated, and that allows the stones to settle and shift more than usual, basically undermining the entire structure. I'd prefer to see the foundation stones begin much deeper and to set them on metal pilings that have been pounded into the earth. And we'll need metal pilings angling back into the hill as well, because if the foundation starts shifting, stones will begin failing, and future generations will not be able to enjoy the beauty you've spent so much effort creating. I believe I can make these stairs withstand almost all the water we can throw at them."

The men stared at me in confusion, and I realized they hadn't understood any of my modern, American-accented French.

"He was educated in Rome," the king told his brother with a little shrug.

So I explained again using my considerable skills at charades, after which Constantine looked sour-faced and the king impressed.

"You will discuss this with Master Garnier," King Lacort said. "I would like his approval. It would be nice to pass this great legacy down through our family for generations to come."

"Or maybe we shouldn't finish it at all," Constantine suggested. "It is a large expense, and don't forget that we will be returning to the capital soon."

The king sighed, and a shadow passed over his face. "Not soon enough. Not until the queen is satisfied of my safety."

I remembered the attempted murder Jianne had mentioned, but it sounded as if maybe it had already happened, which would be good for us as we wouldn't become suspects.

"Are you in danger?" I asked the king.

"Uh . . ." He looked around as if to check to see if the guards were in hearing range, but they'd retreated some distance away after taking their turns in the ditch.

I couldn't blame them for not wanting to stick around to help further. The day was hot for this early in May, and even the steward had seated himself on a large, square-cut stone under a tree near where the horses grazed. He'd removed his hat and sweat dripped from his receding hairline despite the frantic way he fanned himself with his hand.

"There was an attempt on my brother's life at court," Constantine said. "Or more to the point, it happened at the palace in the capital. But it was foiled, and the culprit caught."

King Lacort nodded. "However, my queen believes there is a co-conspirator because the man was murdered in our dungeon before we could question him."

"That was likely a loyal guard seeking revenge on your behalf," Constantine said.

The king sighed. "Perhaps. But generally, guards like prisoners to hang for their crimes."

"Yes, indeed, but you are beloved by your people." Constantine shared a glance with the king. "You need not feel guilt, brother. The prisoner's punishment was adequate, given that he was poisoned with the same arsenic he attempted to use on you."

All this talk of murder was making me uneasy. Had Jianne mistaken the details, or would there still be another incident here? It wasn't like her to get things so wrong. She loved history every bit as much as she enjoyed interior design, both of which she'd learned at her aunt's knee. Could our presence have already changed events? But no, the first attempt had taken place far away from here *before* we stepped back in time, and it was possible the tale had not survived the centuries.

"I am happy the attempt was . . . uh, foiled," I said. Then, more in desperation than with an intention to irritate Constantine, I said, "You mentioned you had access to stone. Is it the same white stone? You weren't, perchance, considering using some of the stone from the walls, were you? Because the walls have some of the best foundations I've seen in Beaumont and also in other countries. I guarantee they will last centuries with minimal issues if we do not upset them."

Constantine gave me a glare of pure hatred before he quickly smoothed his features. "I'm not sure what you are talking about. The stone comes from the quarry, of course."

The king angled a knowing glance at his brother. "See that it does. If we have any intrusions from our neighbors, we will need both strong inner and outer walls."

"Of course, Bérenger," Constantine said, abruptly deferential.

"The foundation will take weeks to complete," I added. Or perhaps longer, depending on how many workers the king could give me and if the blacksmith could forge what I needed.

"We can begin after we discuss the matter with Master Garnier," the king said. "I will send a runner to him in the morning to ask when we may expect him."

That gave me an idea. "If you have paper—parchment—I could draw up the design to send as well."

"An excellent idea." King Lacort met his brother's gaze once more. "My brother is a great one for letter-writing. He can arrange parchment for you."

"Indeed. I will see that it is delivered to your quarters," Constantine said, but not before giving a little roll of his eyes as the king looked away, signaling his doubt that I would be able to do more than a rudimentary drawing. "I look forward to seeing your design."

"I am in your debt." I gave a little bow that hid my amusement at this pompous fool. "It would be convenient to have a large parchment size, if possible. Like you would use with a map."

"That will be more of a challenge, but you will have what you wish by the end of the day." Constantine sounded aggrieved.

"This is all great news," the king said. "The queen will very much enjoy the stairs when they are finished, and so will my son. Come, let us mount up. A few items of business demand my attention at the castle before supper." He gave the lake a final satisfied glance before striding powerfully toward the horses.

Constantine didn't immediately follow but waited a few seconds to say between gritted teeth, "If your intentions regarding my brother are anything but honorable, know that I will have your head on a pike, cousin or no." With that, he hurried after his brother, tripping on a rock that made me notice the three-inch heels on his boots, though they appeared designed to purposefully to hide that fact.

As I rode back to the castle next to the king, I could feel Constantine's gaze digging into me from behind. I wasn't sure what to make of him.

To my relief, the women awaited us in the courtyard, wearing medieval gowns that looked strange but somehow exactly right. Jianne's gown had a rich, gold patterned underdress, with a square-cut neck and long sleeves that widened at the end. An over-dress of deep red and gold fell down the front and back, giving a layered look. Gold also trimmed the dress, making jewelry unnec-essary, though she wore the gold necklace I knew had been her mother's. Because of the square neckline, the dress left a compel-ling amount of skin showing, and I could barely stop myself from gaping.

Constantine was off his horse and in front of the ladies by the time I could find my feet. The queen made the introductions while he slavered over their proffered hands like a groveling dog, particularly Jianne's, who smiled at him as if he didn't look the part of a pampered court jester.

Great, I thought. The king's brother had taken an interest in the woman who held my heart, and there was not a single thing I could do about it.

Chapter 4

Jianne

I was relieved that Emerson appeared unhurt, so he must not have offended anyone too badly while we'd been separated. His clothes were dirty, though, and I wanted to know why, but the king's brother, Constantine, wouldn't stop kissing my hand, so I couldn't move closer to ask.

"Your cousins have been kind enough to bring us some sweets," the queen said to the king. "They are most interesting and desirable. You must try them." She lifted the box of pastries Mel had gifted her while we were trying on our borrowed gowns.

"Must I indeed?" asked King Bérenger. "Well, if you are that impressed, my dear, then let's have at it."

There seemed to be some underlying message there, and I suspected it had something to do with the fact that there were now several pastries missing, as well as parts of others cut off. Sophia had obviously had them tested for poison while we'd been occupied trying on gowns.

Of course I knew the pastries were safe—unless the queen had planted something inside them herself. But no, I'd seen the way she'd looked at her husband, so I watched with only a little trepidation as the king and his brother each bit into one of the pastries with exclamations of delight. At least the brother had to stop groping my hand to eat.

"They are as good as you promised," the king said. "We must have the cook imitate them." He gestured to Emerson. "Please, take one, Lord Selmone. Join us after all your hard work at the lake."

"Oh, enough with Lord this and that," the queen said, waving a hand. "These are our cousins, after all. In private company, we can very well dispense with formalities. Please, call us Sophia and Bérenger."

"Ah, yes." Constantine once again edged closer to me in his ridiculously puffy pants and elaborate hat. His clothing would make even the most outlandish medieval outfit from my aunt's collection look conservative. "I confess that I am quite taken with our cousins and would be happy to address them more familiarly."

A thread of warning shot through me at the tone of his voice, and I had to force myself not to cringe away from him. I was finished cringing from any man for any reason. I might have to pretend to like this pompous fool until we could figure out how to get back to our own time, but I would not let him control me.

"Please do call me Emerson," Emerson told the king, thankfully drawing our attention back to him. "And you as well." He gave Constantine a flat, challenging stare that had me grateful I'd introduced him as my brother. Emerson didn't have the background to understand the atrocities that occurred in these times, and I feared his boldness would get him into trouble.

The king clapped Emerson on the shoulder. "Yes, indeed,

cousin. As I was saying, have one of your excellent sweets. I've half a mind to send word to steal your kitchen staff out from under you."

Sophia extended the box to Emerson, who looked ready to say no, but I nodded ever so slightly. It wasn't a good idea to evoke suspicions about the pastries now. "Thank you," Emerson said, brushing his hands on his pants. "I think I will. I've been looking forward to these for what seems like centuries."

Everyone laughed. "They taste as if they were made this morning," Sophia said, "not traveling for days along your journey."

"I'm sure your cook will be able to recreate them beautifully," I said, avoiding her subtle question. I looked at Mel to help me distract the queen, but Mel appeared faint again, as if going through the time portal had given her an illness that stole all her usual forcefulness and energy. It was a little disconcerting to be the most knowledgeable person in this adventure. I'd become accustomed to receiving support from Mel and Harper as I tested spreading my wings, but now Mel seemed barely aware of her surroundings, and Emerson, well, he was a man, and I was leery of letting myself need him too much.

"If you ladies will excuse Fredrick and me, we have some business to attend to." He looked at his brother. "Come, Constantine."

Constantine took that as his cue to kiss my hand again. "I look forward to rejoining our lovely guests at the evening meal." His hand was moist and his full lips even more so. I vowed to find some gloves as soon as possible.

"I will check on the kitchen staff," Sophia said, placing her hand on the crook of her husband's arm. "Enjoy the rest of your stroll around the grounds. Supper should be ready by the time you return."

The king and queen walked purposefully away, followed by the other two. Constantine tried to give me a meaningful look, but I ignored him and bent to talk to a child who had paused with his mother to stare at me.

"Hi, there," I said.

The boy gave me a little bow, his eyes wide. "Are you a princess?" he asked, his gaze fixing on my dress.

Though my lineage had come down through the same line as the king, and our families had intermingled throughout the ensuing centuries, we were technically removed enough in the future that I didn't hold that official title.

"Nay, lad," I said. "I am naught but a poor relation to the king."

"You are the most lovely lady I ever did see." Turning to look at his mother, he added, "Right, Mum?"

"Aye, boy. That she is." She curtsied to me. "Thank 'ee for your kindness, m'Lady."

"Good morrow," I told them. I looked up to see Emerson staring at me in a way I'd caught him doing before but couldn't quite decipher.

"He's right," Emerson said in English, his face sober. "For a moment there, I thought I'd have to borrow a sword so I could fend off the king's brother. You know, to protect your honor." His grin was back now, and it made my stomach flutter.

"Constantine happens to be our cousin," I reminded him, also reverting to his native tongue.

"Fake cousin, you mean," Mel said, shaking herself out of her distraction. "He's a bottom feeder." She lifted the skirt of her royal blue velvet dress. "Come on. Let's go find a private place to talk."

We walked through the courtyard, where servants, soldiers, peasants, knights, and an assortment of animals made the area much busier than it would be in the future. Two guards from the king's retinue followed us at a distance, and I wasn't sure if it was for our protection or to keep an eye on us.

Mel kept pace with us, and I hoped that meant she was feeling better. "So, where did you go with the king?" she asked Emerson. "We were worried about you."

"To the stairs by the lake, and I'm sorry to report that what they've done there so far isn't even nearly as strong as what we found back in our time. So either it was repaired at a time that wasn't documented, or they will completely rework it when the master mason returns. The way it is now, it won't hold up long enough for us to go through that door in the first place."

For some reason that struck me as amusing. "So we can't go through in the first place because it won't be there, but isn't that a paradox? Shouldn't we just disappear back to where we came from?"

He tapped his chin with his finger in contemplation as if he found my comment fascinating. "You would think, right? But apparently that's not the way it works because here we are."

"Maybe it's not the little room at all," I suggested.

"Exactly." Emerson stepped over a pile of dung that signaled we were approaching the stables near the back entrance. "But we don't actually know that we can't get back or what caused the time shift in the first place. Working on the wall will give us the opportunity to explore what might have triggered it. All we know is that we're here, and that couldn't have happened with the current structure because it won't exist like it was in our time."

"You really think we can get home?" Mel asked eagerly. "Because the idea of spending the rest of my life without Damien is too awful to even think about." The tightness returned to her voice, telling me she was barely holding herself together. Mel had grown up an orphan and had fought her way through life and school all on her own, and this helplessness wasn't at all like her. It made me feel protective of her, because for much of my life, I'd known that feeling only too well.

Emerson nodded firmly. "We'll get back. It if happened once, we know it's possible. And we might as well keep busy while we're stuck here. If we do the work right, it could save us a lot of headaches in the future. And save Tristan and Harper a boatload of money."

"It would be an interesting challenge to engineer," Mel said. For the first time since our arrival, I saw a hint of her normal self.

"It would. And since we don't have access to our computers, it'll have to be old school, by hand. I've already arranged for some paper. Between the two of us, I think we can draw up some basic plans that the king can send for approval while we create more detailed ones. The blacksmith could begin working right away on the metal supports."

Mel tapped the reticule the queen had provided for her. "We can do the calculations on my phone app and copy them over before I lose battery."

"Provided it has offline capability," Emerson said with a slight roll of his eyes.

Mel perked up even more at that challenge. "Even offline, it will cut our hand work by eighty percent."

He stared in exaggerated shock. "Really?"

"It's handy. That's what I keep trying to tell you. And it still has the measurements I took of the stairs at the beginning of the project."

I laughed at Emerson's expression. "Looks like Mel wins the app argument."

"For once, I hope so," Emerson said with feeling. "Regardless, we can at least be sure the stairs will be built to last—and we can make sure the king's weasel of a brother doesn't cannibalize the stones on the inner wall. I'm pretty sure he's the one who ordered that the last time."

"Don't you mean the king's *fop* of a brother?" Mel asked. "Because that's an insult to weasels everywhere."

"Right." Emerson sniggered.

"I thought his clothes were interesting," I said, trying to look sincere.

Emerson rolled his eyes. "That's because you like circus clowns."

We all laughed, falling into silence as we left the courtyard and turned to follow a worn path along the wall, still trailed by our guards. To our right, fields stretched out with peasants bent over them.

I stopped and stared. "We are really in the past. This is probably the most exciting thing that has ever happened to me." Though coming here had an element of danger, it was also strangely empowering. I was centuries away from my father and his influence and from anyone who'd ever known me except these two friends who loved and supported me. I could do anything or be anyone here.

"And the most terrifying," Mel added.

"That too," I said, offering her a smile.

Emerson was quiet, and I let my gaze slide toward him. He was also looking out over the fields, facing in the direction of the lake, probably with a head full of plans. I loved his focus, I loved his personality, and I loved the way he so often stared at me. So why couldn't I trust him with my heart? His not-so-subtle hints regarding his interest in me hadn't become threatening or pushy, and his patience seemed unending. Could all that run out?

No, I couldn't think that way. After so many years of feeling like dirt under my father's shoe, I had to act out of love, not fear. If my mother had lived, life might have been different, and maybe confidence would have come more naturally to me. But there was also the possibility that if I'd had a refuge, I might have become more like him. Maybe she would have been more of a victim. In these moments of clarity, I was glad my mother had been set free from the emotional prison he'd created because I'd seen too many rich, abused children grow up to abuse their families.

"Jianne?"

I blinked to see Emerson watching me with concern. "Yes?"

He hesitated a heartbeat before saying, "I'm wondering what you think of building something more permanent at the top of the lake valley instead of a wooden gazebo, something that might last until our time?"

He had so not been going to say that, I knew, because his heart was in his eyes, and from how tightly his fists clenched at his side, he was keeping his distance only with great effort. Maybe. I wanted to throw my arms around him and ask, but instead I only managed to smile and say, "That's a fantastic idea. It would have to be substantial, maybe even a small building, but it could be done."

"We'd have to widen the landing at the top of the stairs." He looked up at the sky thoughtfully, as if seeing images there. Sometimes when he described what he wanted to create, I was convinced he was a genius. How could his interest in me last?

No. That wasn't constructive, and he didn't deserve the thoughts. Neither of us did.

"I love the idea," Mel said into the silence. "That would be like our modern version of a pool house or lake cottage, or whatever. Much more conducive to a party."

We started walking again, and Emerson began telling us about the poisoning attempt at Beaumont's capital city. "The king seems rather suspicious that the man was killed before questioning," Emerson added, "and he says the queen believes there was an accomplice. He didn't say it outright, but I believe she thinks the man was murdered before he could give up his accomplice's name.

I have to agree. Did you ever read about a poisoning before he arrived here? Could that have been the attempt you talked about?"

"No, definitely not," I said. "It was here, and it was this month because I studied the background when we started renovations. I like to do that when I start a project to get the feel of it all."

He nodded. "Makes sense. We did something similar when we went to visit all the other castles and significant structures in Beaumont. So . . . that means the king will be poisoned sometime within the next three weeks."

"Right. And I only know the king eventually dies at the palace in the city because the text mentions it. Since the death didn't have anything to do with my research on the castle, I didn't really dig into the cause. In school, all we learn is the major events."

"My bet for poisoning is on the king's brother," Emerson said. "Or it would be if he hadn't threatened me regarding his brother's life, and if you hadn't said that he gave up the throne to his nephew when he came of age."

"Wait. Constantine threatened you?" I didn't like the sound of that.

"Only if something happened to the king." Emerson paused to examine a stone in the wall that didn't quite match in color. "This has been repaired, and expertly so. I never caught it in our time because the coloring is the same there now."

"You're right." Mel leaned in to take a brief look before we continued walking.

"Anyway, if the brother gives up the throne to the rightful heir instead of bumping him off too," Emerson said, "then it's likely he didn't kill the king."

I wracked my brain to remember what I'd read but came up with nothing to add. "I think I might have some of the articles still downloaded on my phone." I started reaching for it, but Emerson's next words stopped me.

"Maybe not the best time," he said, casting a glance at our guards. "And, uh, you guys did put your phones on airplane mode, right? To make the batteries last."

Mel and I nodded. "And we turned off all the background apps," I said. "Even so, my phone will barely last through tomorrow, I'm guessing."

That gave us all pause. We were definitely children of the new generation, and I'd already had to prevent myself from checking my phone more than a dozen times.

Before we'd gone much further, a deep gong sounded in the distance, and the guards signaled that it was time to return to the castle.

Emerson muttered under his breath, "Well, since the cannibalized wall is on the other side of the castle, it's not as if we can go check on it now to see if the weasel was messing with it. I'll have to take a horse out later."

Mel laughed. "Take a horse out to check on a castle wall. I never thought I'd hear anyone say those words, much less hear them from you."

Emerson grinned. "Well, when in Rome . . ."

The guards led us to the castle's great hall, where tables filled the space and many knights, soldiers, and peasants gathered for the evening meal. Sophia greeted us with a handsome toddler on her hip. He was a chubby little boy with rosy cheeks, wavy black hair, and large eyes that hinted at the best of both parents' genes. We hadn't met him before, but Sophia had told Mel and me all about him. After fifteen years of marriage, this little boy was the only fruit of their union. They'd almost given up hope of ever having children, and in a dark moment, Sophia had even asked the king to take a new wife, which he'd thankfully refused to do.

"You are just in time," Sophia said. "Did you enjoy your stroll?"

I nodded. "Very much so."

"And who is this?" Emerson's voice went sing-song as he bent to address the little boy.

Sophia set her chin on the boy's head as he pushed his face against her in reaction to Emerson's attention. "This is our son, Prince Matis. Say hello, Matis."

"Hello," said the boy after a bit more urging, his smile shy and beautiful.

For a few minutes, Emerson engaged the child in silly conversation that had us all laughing, until the thin steward came and whisked Emerson away, muttering something about proper clothing.

"My, your brother is so charming," Sophia said. "It's a wonder he isn't married yet."

"I've wondered that myself," I said.

Mel elbowed me, and I knew why. She'd been urging me to open myself to Emerson, and I kept saying he was just a friend. Yes, I'd noticed that he'd recently slowed down with his constant dating, though women still contacted him regularly. But what did that have to do with me?

Sophia led us to a dais where the king's table was set. Steaming dishes that I knew would be mostly meat awaited us, but the king and his courtiers were not yet in sight. "You'll eat up here with us as our honored guests," Sophia said. "You can't know what it is for me to have you both here." She put a hand on Mel's arm. "How are you holding up, dear? I had the cook make something special for you. It should calm your stomach. It always did when I was expecting."

"Expecting?" Mel's voice came out as a squeak.

I stared, barely able to stop my jaw from dropping, and the pieces snapped into place. Mel wasn't just feeling weird because of the time shift—there was something a lot more important going on.

"Yes, I guessed," Sophia said in answer to Mel's obvious surprise. She reached to squeeze Mel's hand. "Don't worry yourself. We have the best physician here in the castle, and when you're ready to see him, I will arrange an examination."

A servant caught Sophia's eyes. "Oh, it appears I need to get this little prince to his governess. Sit anywhere you'd like in this section. I'll be right back." She hurried off, shifting her son's weight on her ample hip.

That left me alone with Mel. I looked around to be sure no one was listening. "You're going to have a baby?"

Mel gave a hesitant nod.

"How long have you known?"

"Since this morning." She sighed and reached out to grip a high-backed chair. "And Damien doesn't know yet. He was gone with Tristan before I got up. I didn't even tell him I was taking a test because I didn't think there was any way I could be . . . well, I'd just been feeling a little off, so I took it to reassure myself. I've never been very regular."

"But it's wonderful news!" I hugged her. "I mean, I know it's scary too, but it's more wonderful than anything. When Damien hears, he'll be doing summersaults of joy. And his mother will be even happier."

"If I ever get to tell them."

I sucked in a breath. For a moment, I'd forgotten our little problem of having no idea how we'd get home. No wonder Mel was so distraught. The idea of Damien never holding their child, of raising a baby alone in the Middle Ages, was terrifying.

She leaned against me the way she leaned into Emerson earlier. I tightened my arms around her. "We will get home," I whispered fiercely. "We will. I promise."

I didn't know how I'd make it happen, but there had to be

some kind of archive at the castle. Tonight while Mel and Emerson drafted the plans for the lake stairs, I would research all mentions of odd things happening in the region. Someone had to know what had happened to us and how to reverse it.

Chapter 5

Emerson

Supper was torture. Trying to understand all the ancient French made me crazy, and having to watch Constantine fawn all over Jianne made me want to punch something. Hard. Preferably his handsome face. The man took every opportunity to touch her hand or lean in close, and I could do nothing but watch from my seat between her and Mel. My only comfort was that despite Jianne's earlier defense of his attire, she avoided his touches as much as possible and talked to him in stiff but polite tones, exactly how she'd treated her father the one time I'd seen them together. Of course, she treated me that way sometimes too, and I was a lot less pushy than either of those jerks.

Mel also had me worried. I knew my best friend, and something more than time travel was upsetting her. I couldn't wait until I got her alone to question her.

If not for those two worries, I might have enjoyed the banquet and the entertainment. We had eight kinds of savory meats and endless refills of delicious sweet mead. A juggler, a bard, a contortionist, and even a fire-eater took turns showing us what I assumed was typical medieval entertainment. Quite amazing, actually.

But I would have traded it all to have one good punch at Constantine.

Finally, the king excused himself, and the servants began removing the remnants of the meal.

Mel drew me away from the table. "What is wrong with you? You look angry."

My eyes drifted to where Constantine was standing near the queen, bidding Jianne good night. I dragged my gaze back to Mel. "I could say the same about you. Why did they bring you milk instead of mead? And how come you got so many assortments of breads when the rest of us were offered mostly meat?"

Her eyes closed briefly, and when they opened, they were filled with tears. "I'm pregnant. I just found out this morning. And ever since we came through that wormhole or whatever it's called, I am getting more and more nauseated. I don't know how much comes from the baby or how much is from worrying that we won't get back."

Shock reverberated through me, and it took a moment for her words to sink in. Then I picked her up and twirled her around. "Oh, Mel, that's wonderful! I mean about the baby, of course, not being sick. And it's going to be okay. We will make it okay. And when we do, Damien will owe me big time. Maybe he'll give me one of his houses or vineyards. Or maybe you can name the little guy after me."

That made her laugh, as I'd known it would. "Thanks," she said. "But seriously, if we don't . . ."

I sobered. "I'll take care of you, Mel. You and the baby. Always. You know that."

"I do know." She glanced over to where Constantine was

finally taking his leave of Jianne and the queen. "And I know why you're out of sorts too. But you don't have to worry. Jianne sees right through him."

I hoped so, but the fact that she might not hurt too much for me to even say the words.

"Come on," I said. "Constantine said he had the paper and writing utensils taken to my quarters, wherever those are. Let's get to work on those plans. You help me start with that app of yours, and then you can sleep while I bang them out."

"I'm not an invalid," she protested. "And I'm looking forward to getting my mind off everything."

"Right. Then I won't say anything about you looking like you're half asleep on your feet."

Mel rolled her eyes and punched my arm half-heartedly. "Let's go."

Jianne and the queen stepped toward us with a servant standing behind them. "I'll have Claude show you to your rooms," Sophia said. "The castle can be a little confusing the first few days, especially in the far wing where you are staying. They are the nicest rooms since we renovated them first, but they are rather far from the main part of the castle."

I was relieved to know that it appeared I would be in the same wing as the women. I wondered if there were locks on the doors because I wouldn't put it past Constantine to make a surprise visit to Jianne's quarters.

"Thank you again for your gracious welcome," Jianne said.

Sophia's smile widened. "Nonsense, I am pleased to have you. Maybe we can go riding tomorrow or have a picnic. But for now, I'm needed in the nursery. His Little Highness won't fall asleep unless I tell him a story."

"That reminds me," Jianne said. "Do you have a library?"

"Library?" Sophia looked puzzled.

"Archives. Books."

Sophia's face lit up. "Oh, yes, that's what we call them, though I have heard the other term, and I think I will adopt it. Library sounds so deliciously modern. After all, we are nearing the end of the century." She laughed. "Collecting books is my hobby. Though most of the books we have here are local histories rather than the wider assortment we have at the palace or in the monasteries." She leaned forward and whispered, "Which actually has made them more interesting to me." Louder, she added, "Are you a fellow reader? I have even transcribed a few books I love, though I'm not as fast as the monks, and I cannot illustrate at all. But you are welcome to borrow any book in our archives. Claude will show you there too."

"Hankering for a romance?" I asked Jianne, reverting once more to English as the servant led us to the library on the second floor.

"No," she replied in the same language. "I'm trying to find stories about time travel. We know it happened, and local histories may give us some clue as to how."

"That doesn't mean anyone has admitted to time traveling in one of the books," Mel said. "Or written about how to do it. Maybe that little room is only a one-way trip, and we'll never—"

"Don't say it." Jianne put her hand on Mel's shoulder. "We'll find a way."

The servant stopped and bowed with a flourish at a set of double doors, both of which were propped open. "Brother Francis is inside and can help you with any requests. With his blessing, the curses will not harm you, even if you remove the books from the archive."

"Curses?" I said in a voice so low the servant wouldn't understand even if he spoke modern English.

Jianne laughed quietly. "They write out dire curses on the last pages to prevent stealing in case the monk or whoever is watching over the library nods off or something."

"I see. That's funny," I said. "But if you go in there asking for histories involving time travel, isn't that going to sound suspicious to the monk? You sure you don't want us to go in with you?" My protective urges were apparently working overtime, but seeing as I'd spent the past eight months actively pursuing her, and we were currently stuck in the past, I allowed myself a little leeway.

She gave me a slow smile that made my insides burn with something that definitely wasn't brotherly. "Thanks, but I think I can handle a monk. You guys go do some engineering, and I'll meet you in your room after I get what I need. Since Sophia said I can borrow the books, I'm guessing they aren't chained down the way they are in some medieval libraries."

A few minutes later, Mel and I were in my room, which she said appeared to be a cut-down version of the suite she and Jianne shared down the hall. A crackling fire burned in the fireplace, as if waiting for us, and a large banquet table had been set up, running the length of the far wall beyond the bed. In the middle of the table sat a sturdy, eight-candle candelabra, only one of which was currently lit. Surrounding that, at a safe distance, we found a stack of oversized parchment, a handful of quills, several bottles of ink, two knives, a long, metal, ruler-like straight edge, and, more surprisingly, the medieval versions of a math compass and protractor.

"Oh, boy," Mel said, chuckling. "This brings back memories of those hands-on classes we took sophomore year."

"You can say that again. Wonder what the knives are for, though."

"No idea. But look at the candles. How quaint. We'll have to light more to see properly."

She sat down on the uncomfortable-looking loveseat and drew

out her phone as I began lighting the candles and laying out the paper that wasn't nearly enough for the mess-ups that were usually rampant in hand work. We'd have to be careful.

"Why don't you work on the types of metal reinforcements we'll need for the blacksmith to copy while I start on the stair design?" Mel said. "And the plans don't need to be perfect. We just need something to show the master mason, right? To make sure they do a decent foundation. I have the measurements here, but we'll have to double-check the length before the actual build—or he will."

"Okay." As the room was overwarm, I pulled off my tunic, leaving on the undershirt and rolling up the long, slightly puffy sleeves so I wouldn't get ink on the material.

It took me awhile to get the hang of the quills and ink, and I destroyed two of the parchments in the meantime, but I completed my support designs before she finished the initial staircase plans on her phone app. Then she rang the servant bell to ask for more candles and a snack, which she nibbled on cautiously while we discussed the project and agreed on one major and two minor adjustments. By now, she was looking rather green, so I sent her back to the couch to rest as I made the changes on her app. It was a far cry from my computer program, but it was much better than doing it all by hand. I'd have to give this win to Mel.

"I'll do the paper copy," I said, after we reviewed the designs a final time. "You should lie down on the bed and take a nap." I'd actually have to copy it twice because I wanted a spare on hand and the phone battery would soon die. If I brought that up, though, Mel would insist on doing her share, and she looked beat. With Damien not here to protect her, that job fell to me, her best friend.

"Well, you were always better at doing the hand drawings," she said, stifling a yawn. "And I'm cold anyway. Looks like our fire is about to burn out." She rubbed her arms through the material of her dress.

Now that she mentioned it, I was chilly, so I laid a log from the nearby stack onto the fire, careful to use the metal tongs on the hot gate. A gas fireplace with its two little switches was so much easier.

"Do you think Jianne should be back yet?" I asked as Mel climbed under the blanket. She'd been gone for more than three hours, but it was only the past hour that anxiety had begun to knot in my stomach.

Mel opened an eye. "You have to let her make choices, Emerson. All her life, she's been surrounded by controlling people who made her feel worthless or well-meaning people who blamed her for not fixing the problem. She is a strong woman inside, and she just needs time to realize that."

"I know at least a little about her crappy father and the rest of her family who couldn't help," I said, standing to face her. "Not even her aunt, who is more than a decent person. But that's not the woman I know. The Jianne I know isn't submissive at all or begging me to give her an opinion. I know she is perfectly capable, but I also know that she won't let me in. She doesn't ask for help. What if she never trusts me or another man? Or anyone really? That's a lonely way to live. People need to rely on people and be relied on."

"Give her time," Mel said cryptically and closed her eyes once again.

I fumed a bit as I worked because why should I have to pay for the sins of others? But my fury died as I thought about the past eight months of wooing—or trying to woo—Jianne. It hadn't been unpleasant, not by a long shot, and the truth was that I would wait another year or even five if it meant eventually winning her heart and helping her see the woman I saw every time

I looked at her. But there was also the very real possibility that she would never see me as more than a friend, and since I couldn't change that, there might come a time when I'd have to set her free completely by returning to the States.

I'd started the second draft of drawings and was debating going to find Jianne when a knock on the door propelled me from my seat. To my relief, it was Jianne accompanied by a servant, their arms full of heavy, hand-bound tomes. I moved my finished drawings aside and helped them set down the books.

"So," I said casually once the servant was gone, "did the monk bore you with fifteen generations of histories?"

Her dark eyes gleamed with amusement. "Actually, yes. But it helped me narrow down what I needed. He told me a few strange stories that might be related." She stopped talking and picked up one of my drawings that showed a close-up of a section of the room beneath the stairs. "Wow, it doesn't even look like you did this by hand."

I laughed. "Look closer, and you'll see the blots I made with the quill, unfortunately, but I did take a calligraphy class at some point in college, so it turned out better than I expected."

She peered closer. "Obviously. You could have been an illustrator for one of these medieval books. Or at least you could make a handwritten copy of a text. Open that top one there, and you'll see."

I opened the fancy hand-bound tome and was greeted with a drawing of a tree designed with elaborate flourishes, followed by sentences of calligraphy in neat, tiny rows. "No way could I do this."

"Yes, you could." She laid down my drawing, pulled a sheet of parchment off the much-reduced stack, and began making strong, sure strokes with the quill, using a knife to hold the parchment in place as she worked. I shut the book and moved to stand beside her, watching a small building come to life under her able fingers.

"Why the knife?" I asked.

"To keep oils off the parchment. And less smearing. But don't worry if you didn't do it. They won't need these plans for long, after all. The knife is also used for sharpening the quills, but it looks like we have plenty, and they are well made." She worked awhile longer in silence while I watched. I'd seen plenty of sketches she'd made for her interior decorating, and I knew she was talented, but this drawing showed me that she also understood at least some of the principles of building design.

"You'll have to put in the dimensions," she said, darting a glance at me. "I have no idea what size it can be, though I guess that depends on how large you made the landing."

"It's much better than I envisioned," I said. "I like that rooftop courtyard."

She grinned. "I think they might be able to see the whole lake from it. Sophia will like being able to keep an eye on her son when he's out there in a boat."

"Speaking of the queen," I said. "Mel said she guessed about the baby. Does she know that Mel's married? And if so, how come it isn't a bad idea for Mel to be married?"

"Because Damien's not around to be bumped off so some other noble can claim Mel." Jianne bent closer to the table as she added detail to her drawing. "But to be fair, there really are only a handful of nobles here, and they're all knights sworn to protect the king. Mostly I think the lack of the usual hangers-on is because Sophia is worried about the poisoning. But as far as medieval rulers go, I think Bérenger is a good man, and if we don't somehow incur disfavor, he'll protect us."

"I like him," I agreed. "But not his brother."

She didn't respond to that but said instead, "Anyway, to answer your question, the queen noticed Mel's wedding ring and asked about it."

I leaned closer to watch her add a pattern of stone to the exterior blocks. "They used wedding rings in the fourteenth century?"

"Yes. In Beaumont during the ceremony, the husband-to-be puts the ring on different fingers—his wife's, of course—and repeats phrases said by the priest. The last one is on the wedding finger, the same one we use today. Once it gets there, they're married."

I chuckled. "Sounds interesting."

She stood, and suddenly we were very close, so close that all my senses sprang into overdrive. Each familiar curve of her face beckoned, and my hand seemed to have a life of its own as I reached toward her. Here we were, two weeks after my first kiss attempt at her aunt's, and I might just give into the temptation to try again. If I did, would she laugh and move away?

But she stood like a statue as my hand cupped her cheek, my thumb just grazing the three freckles under her right eye. Our eyes locked. My breath caught, and my heart pounded in my chest, seeming to ring in my ears. Frozen, I waited for a sign to know if this was okay. The last thing I wanted to do was to push her away.

Moments ticked by.

Finally, she put her hand over mine, squeezing softly as she brought it from her face down to rest on the table. She left her hand on mine as she said, "If I had to be stuck in the past with anyone, it would be you, Emerson."

"And why's that?" I didn't dare move for fear she'd withdraw her hand.

"Because you make me laugh, and you have a tendency to be positive even when things look bleak." Her seductive smile sent more heat through me. "And because we're friends, of course. Your friendship means more to me than you know."

The words were like a bucket of ice water on my raging desire to kiss her. I was a friend. Always a friend with her.

Fighting disappointment, I leaned forward, refusing to let her take the easy way out. Her eyes widened as I kissed her on the cheek near her ear.

"I care about you, too," I said softly. "And since I'm an honorable man, maybe you should go back to your room before I forget that I am supposed to be your brother."

Chapter 6

Jianne

I sucked in a breath as Emerson moved away from me, pulling his hand out from under mine. Why had I panicked when all I wanted to do was to kiss him? Every time I thought that maybe I could be the loving person I was in my dreams with him, my stomach clenched, and I pulled away.

Or called him a friend.

I knew what being a *friend* meant to him. It meant the way he felt for Mel and Harper, and that was not how I thought about him. Why couldn't I simply let things go a little bit longer between us? Just for once?

Emerson sauntered to the bed and placed a hand on Mel's shoulder. "Hey," he said softly, "you need to wake up."

Without moving, she mumbled something I didn't hear.

"Sorry, can't," he said. "If this were any other place, I'd grab a blanket and curl up with you, but I don't think they'd understand that here, even if I'm supposedly your brother. And I'm pretty sure Damien wouldn't be okay with it, even though he trusts you. We kinda aren't kids anymore."

Mel blinked as she came to a sitting position, smoothing her blue dress with both hands. "Man, this thing is beautiful but so uncomfortable to sleep in. The seams hit me in all the wrong places. How long have I been out?"

"Long enough that I've finished the basic drawings," Emerson told her. "Mostly. I still need to copy a few more, or at least the measurements, to make sure we have what we need in case we're here longer than a few days and end up building it ourselves."

Mel groaned. "Of course we need a backup and maybe even more than one. We won't be able to simply print them out if the workers lose a copy."

"Leave it to me," Emerson insisted. "You need to go to bed so you can grow my godchild."

His comment made Mel grin. "Godchild, huh?"

"Of course I'll be the godfather. Damien doesn't have a brother, and after this little trip, it's definitely official that I'm your brother."

They slid from the bed, chuckling, and it made me feel a bit jealous that I wasn't the one having a baby whose life Emerson could be a part of. Emerson sat at the table and pulled a blank sheet toward him, his eyes avoiding me.

"I can help copy the designs," I said.

Mel grabbed a paper and a quill. "We'll all do them. Emerson, show us where you left off. Come on, people. Move."

I couldn't help smiling. Even though Mel was essentially ordering me around, I didn't feel threatened because I'd volunteered to help. Besides, if I changed my mind and walked out, she wouldn't hate me tomorrow or ignore me for a week until I begged forgiveness. She was a true friend.

So was Emerson. He might be avoiding my gaze right now, but in a few minutes, he'd be back to teasing me as if nothing odd had happened between us. And something had happened. I'd rejected him. Again. He was giving us both time to readjust to friendship after my mixed signals.

"I changed our metric measurements to those they use based on what's here on this straight edge and compass, but you should double-check my calculations. I've also included our measurements and made a yardstick with one of the parchments, so the master mason can understand where we're coming from."

"I didn't even think of that," Mel said. "I'll check those first."

Emerson handed me a parchment with a drawing of the lowest section of the stairs. "You can start here," he said, meeting my gaze briefly before finding a sheet for Mel.

"Wait." Mel reached for the drawing I'd done earlier. "Is this the building for the landing? It's perfect. Just a minute and I'll have the measurements I think will work for it. Then Emerson can check those while I double-check his equivalents."

"Sounds good." I slid a blank parchment from the stack and went to sit near the books from the library. I couldn't help pausing a moment to run a finger across the top book, my heart giving a little jump at how perfect it was—how perfect they all were—so new and undamaged. Many of these books wouldn't stand the test of time, and I wished that I could somehow take them all back with me. Or even a single one. And I'd also love to keep the beautiful dress I was wearing. My aunt would love it.

Emerson glanced over to see me fingering the books. "So," he said as if there had been no tension between us, "you mentioned the monk had an interesting story?"

"Oh, yes." I picked up the straight edge to start copying his drawing. "Apparently, there have been several people who have disappeared in the region, never to be seen again. Most were

employed by the castle, but there was a noblewoman who disappeared on a walk by the lake."

"Where? Our lake?" Mel asked.

"They don't know exactly. She was being courted by two men,
and they were on a picnic at the top of the lake valley, and the men
got into a fight. She tried to stop them by grabbing a hand rake or
something from a peasant who was tending a nearby garden, but
they ignored her, so she stormed off down the valley. Both she and
the rake went missing. They think she must have drowned or was
abducted by a bandit who needed a wife."

Mel made a face. "Yikes."

"And there were other stories of disappearing people," I
continued.

"Were they all the same?" Emerson asked. "No one ever came
back?"

I shook my head. "Someone did. A woodsman, in fact. And
he came back wearing odd pants that sound a lot like a pair of
blue jeans."

A tiny sound— a mix between a cry and a laugh—came from
Mel, who had stopped tapping on her phone,. Tears started in her
eyes. "Blue jeans," she muttered. "That's great. Then we may not
be stuck here."

"Right. We just need to find out what the common denom-
inator is." I drew another line, and for a moment, we all worked
in silence. Then I added, "Oh, and there might be someone who
can help us."

Both Emerson and Mel looked at me eagerly. "Who?" Mel
urged.

I chewed on my lower lip. "Well, the local witch. That is, if
we don't get hung for going to see her because witchcraft is illegal
here."

"Great," Mel said. "Just great."

Emerson's eyes glimmered with amusement. "I've always wanted to meet a real witch."

"She's likely just an herbal practitioner," I told them. "Magic isn't real."

He lifted his brows. "Except when it takes you back in time seven and a half centuries. Then I suppose it exists." He paused and added in a sexy drawl, "And then there's the magic between Mel and Damien, and also Harper and Tristan. Anyone who can win Mel and Harper's hearts had to be using magic." These last words were for Mel, but he was looking at me. I held his gaze, determined not to show its compelling effect on me. Because magic was exactly what I felt with him.

Mel laughed. "You can say that again. I am totally under Damien's spell." She said it so casually as if it didn't terrify her. I guess that meant she trusted her husband.

"So we go see the witch," I said, finally pulling my eyes from Emerson to focus on my parchment. "I'll do a little subtle inquiry to see where she lives. But let me do it. I wouldn't want Emerson accidentally asking the servants for a magic spell."

"We could use one to get rid of the king's annoying brother," he mumbled.

I laughed. "I confess that I did get rather tired of him telling me about his castle in the south and all his riches."

"Ha! I knew you hated him." Satisfaction laced Emerson's voice.

"He gives me the creeps," I admitted. In fact, sitting next to Constantine at dinner had been worse than I'd let on to either of my friends. His gaze had unsettled me in a way that I'd only felt before around my father, though for a different reason. I hadn't backed down, but it had been a struggle not to flee.

"Well, he seems quite taken with you," Mel said. "Even Sophia noticed."

I wrinkled my nose. "One more reason to finish these plans so we can get researching. The sooner we all get home, the better."

Even with all of us working hard and using minimum details, it took another two hours to finish all the drawings to Emerson's satisfaction. "Well, these would never pass muster back home," he said finally, "but they're thorough for this day and age."

Mel snorted. "They'll be blown away with them. Whoever this master mason guy is, he isn't Michelangelo."

"I've seen his work," Emerson said. "He might be just as talented."

"If you say so." Mel laid her head on her folded arms that rested on the table, shutting her eyes. "How long do you think it'll be before the master mason returns? I mean, if the king sends these in the morning. Or rather today since half the night is already gone."

"No idea." Emerson began gathering up the plans whose ink was already dry. "But they said he'd be returning shortly."

"Which in the fourteenth century means weeks or even months," I said.

Emerson blew out a long breath. "Well, that doesn't mean we can't leave. At least the master mason will have a copy of the plans in case we figure out how to disappear before he returns."

"If he'll use them." Mel opened her eyes and yawned widely.

"Oh, he'll use them. They're brilliant." Emerson stepped closer to her. "Come on. Let's get you to your room. I'll walk you both there."

I was going to protest but didn't because I hated the thought of being caught by Constantine at this time of night with only Mel for protection. My supposed stature as Constantine's cousin meant he couldn't attack me openly, but he could threaten my friends to force a clandestine affair. Worse, he could attempt to push me into an unwanted marriage, an idea that curdled my blood. It was the very thing I'd worried about when I claimed that

Emerson was my brother because some men weren't above making a woman a widow to clear the way, even without a king's support.

So did my fears regarding Constantine mean he also wasn't above fratricide? Emerson seemed to think that Constantine was protective of his brother, but in my experience, a man's unpleasantness extended into all areas of his life, not just one, and I didn't trust him.

I riffled through the books, choosing my favorites to take with me. Emerson lifted his hands in a silent offer, and I gave him the books and loaded up on the rest. At our suite, Emerson deposited the books on a table and excused himself, giving a little bow that would have tickled my aunt. His gaze brushed mine as clearly as his hand had stroked my cheek earlier, but there was no reproach in his eyes.

"I bet you wish you'd never heard of Beaumont," Mel said, walking him to the door. "I'm really sorry for bringing you here to look for my sister and getting you into all this."

Emerson shook his head. "No, I'm the one who's sorry. You should never have come down to the lake this afternoon. That was my idea."

"I'm the one who saw the door," I offered.

He turned to look at me and arched a brow in that way that I loved. "And I'm the one who opened it. So we're back to me again."

"Whichever way we look at it, we're in this together," I said.

He didn't respond except to say, "Lock your door, okay? I'll see you both in the morning."

Maybe he was remembering my friend comment. And so what if he was? We *were* friends, weren't we?

Mel shut the door behind him and turned to look at me. "What's wrong?" she asked. "You're acting weird, and so is he. Did something happen between you two that I missed?"

I sighed. "Maybe. He . . . I think he might have wanted to kiss me."

Mel snorted. "Well, duh. Everyone knows how Emerson feels about you." She stepped toward me, motioning to the back of her dress. "Can you get this undone? I'd rather not call our lady's maid from her bed."

I began unfastening the numerous small buttons. "I told Sophia we wouldn't need help. And she was fine with it. She's less stuffy than I imagined a queen from this era might be."

"The country probably goes through that stuffy phase later." Mel pulled off the dress and took it to the wardrobe before stripping off the underskirt. "So what did you do when he tried to kiss you?"

I considered what to say as I reached for one of the two nightdresses someone had laid out on a chair. Since I'd read that people in the medieval ages sometimes didn't wear anything to bed, I was happy to see them, though they basically looked like a sheet gathered high around the neck.

I turned so she could unfasten my dress. "I told him he was a good friend."

Mel snorted a laugh. "Good for you." Then she sobered. "But you *are* going to have to make a decision about him eventually. Emerson deserves to find someone who can love him."

"Lots of women love him." There might be a touch of bitterness in my words toward all those women who constantly flirted with him at any function we attended.

"You know what I mean." Mel circled me, taking my hands in hers. "Look, I've known Emerson a very long time, and for many years I wished I could love him romantically. It just wasn't there for us."

"I know, but . . ."

She nodded. "You want to make it on your own—your career,

your relationships, and everything in between. I get it. And if that's what you need, do it. I know you've been through a lot, and you'll get nothing but support from me. But remember that Emerson is one of the good ones. If you don't feel it'll work, you should free him."

My stomach clenched. "I'm not stopping him from leaving."

Mel looked at me for a long moment before saying simply, "Okay. If you say so. But whatever happens or doesn't happen between you two, I'm still going to be your friend." She stifled a yawn. "I guess I need to get to bed. I'm exhausted." She headed toward the bed through the nearest adjoining doorway.

"Hey, Mel," I called.

She paused, looking over her shoulder. "Yes?"

"How did you know you could trust Damien with your heart?" The words cost me to say because I didn't want to be at that point yet. I could see that this new person inside me was going to be quite strong, and I didn't want to go back to depending on anyone else.

Mel turned, her mouth curving in a smile. "I couldn't stop thinking about him, and I made every excuse to be with him. I couldn't imagine my life without seeing him every day." She paused before adding, "I also saw that he was an honorable man, and that helped me take the first step."

Honorable. Just tonight, Emerson claimed to be honorable, and I knew him to be such, at least on the friend level. I hadn't dared to find out anything more.

Mel laughed. "Damien's also incredibly sexy to me. I think that's every bit as important as friendship and trust. Anyway, I'm guessing you already know how you feel about Emerson. But with what you've been through, that still doesn't mean your decision is going to be easy. And it also doesn't mean that he's the only man out there who could make you feel all those things. Timing is also important in a relationship. Good night. I'll see you in the morning."

I stared after her. Did I already know how I felt about Emerson? I loved his company, yes, but I loved us just as we were. It was easy and simple, and I didn't have to worry about, well, anything deeper. I trusted him for where we were now, but not enough to let him have control of any portion of my happiness. I'd promised myself that would always be true with any of my relationships, but now I realized I might be wrong. If I didn't give him more of myself, how would I know if I could trust him with that bit of my soul? And if we didn't exchange soul bits, then how could we create an entire lifetime together?

I gave a long sigh. Whatever else she'd said, Mel had one thing right. If I wasn't interested in Emerson romantically, I had to do more to discourage him. Because he was ready to move forward with finding a wife and having a family, and it was selfish of me to want to keep him where he was without any promise of a future.

But I didn't want to let him go. I hadn't even kissed him yet.

I sucked in a breath, holding it until my emotions calmed. I knew I'd never sleep now, so it was better to lose myself in the very difficult task of deciphering ancient French, which for some reason, was a lot more difficult than the spoken language that we all seemed to magically understand.

Magically.

There was that word again. I couldn't help wondering if maybe this entire experience was only a vivid dream, and maybe tomorrow I'd wake up in my own bed, or maybe in my guest room at Tristan's castle. Strangely, a sharp pang of disappointment shot through me at the thought. For as worrisome as this whole thing was, it was the adventure of a lifetime, and I wouldn't miss it for anything.

Taking the top book from the small ornate table where we'd

set them, I went to the bed in the second room and tucked myself between the silky sheets. It was unusual for us to have been given so much space, as sharing a bed with one's sister in this era certainly wouldn't be odd. I could only assume this was a family suite, perhaps meant for a couple and their children.

A flame still burned in the fireplace, but the room was notably chill now that I'd kicked off my shoes and was wearing only the nightgown. The bed itself was a sinfully soft feather topper over a wool-stuffed mattress, and I hadn't turned many pages before my eyelids drooped.

Then a thought came to me, and I sat up, instantly awake. There was something else I needed to read tonight before my phone's battery drained completely. I needed to know how Sophia's little boy became king, even though Constantine could have so easily had him killed after his father's death.

I reached for the small reticule I'd set on a bedside table before settling back under the warm covers. I skimmed through PDF articles I'd downloaded or stories I'd taken screenshots of until I found the one I was looking for.

Constantine Lacort had died of a mysterious illness a year after his nephew's coronation at age twenty. While Constantine had married during his time as regent, there had been no children. One author theorized that he'd seemed to suffer the same problems that caused his brother to father only one child. There were few details about the illness that killed him, though cancer was a likely culprit as Constantine had been repeatedly treated by a physician for coughing, stomach pains, and swallowing difficulties.

"He died," I said alone in the quiet room, "and he was probably sick for a very long time before he gave up being regent. And I bet that's really why he gave up the throne."

So maybe Constantine did poison his brother but became sick before he could kill his nephew. It was at least possible.

My drowsiness had vanished completely, so I returned to thumbing through the book, finishing it and four more, searching for clues to the time travel and alternately stewing over Constantine's possible role in the king's upcoming death.

My last thought, however, before I drifted off to sleep in the middle of a book wasn't about time travel or Constantine but about Emerson.

I should have let him kiss me.

Chapter 7

Emerson

I was up at first light, having slept only a few restless hours in a bed that wasn't firm enough to support my weight. After dressing again in last night's clothing, I found myself longing for my own jeans and the dirt-streaked T-shirt that was far more comfortable than the long-sleeved one I wore under my tunic, which scratched at the seams. I was sure Constantine must have had a hand in choosing my attire just to put me in my place.

There was no mirror in the room, so I wet my hands from the pitcher of water that sat on the dresser and raked my hands through my hair. Oh, what I wouldn't give for a hot shower! Finally, I emerged into the hallway, asking the first servant I saw where I could find the king. I was taken to the reception room, where, according to my dying phone, I waited an hour before I was given an audience.

"Good morrow," the king called, gesturing me closer to the

fancy, carved table where he sat with his brother and the steward. "I hear you've brought us a drawing?"

"Indeed," I said, striding to the table with my stack of twenty drawings. "I am accustomed to different measurements," I told them as I began spreading out the parchments. "The master mason will want to check the calculations, of course. I have included my original measurements and a guide for him to compare. Maybe start here." I handed him a drawing from a bird's eye view that showed the overall design from the building on the wide landing at the top to the bottom stairs, where a second landing stretched to the water so they could launch boats.

The king perused the drawings, a smile spreading across his wide face. "These are quite detailed. I daresay I am impressed, my cousin."

Constantine's reaction was even more pronounced as he gaped in disbelief. "You did all this in one night?" His eyes met mine angrily as if I'd committed a personal offense.

I shrugged. "Knowing we were pressed for time, my sisters aided me. They are quite skilled at drawing." I tapped the parchment showing the entire stairway. "Jianne thought the queen would enjoy watching the boats from a comfortable building at the top of the valley. It could also be used for housing extra guests when needed."

I continued to explain the design in my limited French, using the detailed drawings of each section to punctuate the words. When I was finished, the king gathered the parchments together and handed them to his steward. "The building at the top of the valley shall be an anniversary gift for my wife. Please send these by rider to the master mason for his approval. If he agrees to the design, we can have the other masons start before he arrives."

The steward rolled the designs into another parchment, setting it with a seal. "I will send them immediately, and we should hear back by late afternoon." He looked at Constantine. "If I may borrow your man and his remarkable steed?"

Constantine nodded agreeably enough, but his mouth twisted in disgust. I had the distinct feeling he'd be one of those old men who looked angry even when they weren't.

"While I'm here, I'd like to take a look at the inner and outer castle walls, if you don't mind," I told the king. "Could I borrow a horse?" Now that the plans were out of my hands, I was back to thinking about ways to keep the king's brother from cannibalizing the stone on the inner and outer walls. If I was successful, maybe Tristan and Harper wouldn't have to invest so much money and time in future repairs.

"Indeed, indeed," the king said with a flourish of his hand. "My stable is yours. Do you need someone to guide you?"

"I think I can find my way." I dared guess that since beginning the repairs in the twenty-first century, I'd studied the castle and its walls more than both men put together.

"Very well. Carry on." The nod was my dismissal.

Bowing, I made a quick retreat, only to find Jianne in the hallway, pacing, a package under her arm. "There you are," she said. "You took long enough in there. I was surprised you weren't in your room."

Not wanting to waste time complaining about the sagging bed, I shrugged. "I wanted to get the plans to the master mason in case we—" I looked around to be sure we weren't being overheard. "In case we find our way back this morning."

"Good idea."

"We do need to decide who to give the other plans to in case the first set gets lost." It wasn't the workers I was worried about right now but Constantine and the unknown rider.

"Sophia," Jianne said. "She'll be the best person. I'll tell her about them." Standing on tiptoe, she reached over with one hand

and brushed the top of my hair with her fingers. "Let me just . . . Not sure what you did with your hair, but it's a little crazy."

"It's called no mirror or shampoo." Her touch felt so good that I had to stop my eyes from closing.

She laughed. "Hey, are you up to going on a little visit with me right now? Mel's upstairs puking, so I ordered her some food and escaped to let her sleep a little more. After the late night, she won't be ready at least until after lunch, which I've had made for us to take, by the way." She placed her pleasantly heavy package in my hands. Since I hadn't eaten breakfast yet, my stomach took that moment to growl at the mere thought of food.

"Poor Mel," I said. "I was planning to check out the inner walls to make sure they aren't still cannibalizing them, but that can wait. I'd be glad to go with you. And food sounds good."

"You haven't eaten breakfast?" Jianne's dark eyes were amused. "There's plenty here if you want it. Or better yet, let's go to the kitchen."

I let her lead me outside and through the already bustling courtyard in the direction of the kitchen. "I have permission to grab a horse," I told her. "I'm sure that includes you."

Jianne laughed. "Sophia already sent someone to the stables to saddle up for us."

"You were that sure you'd find me?"

"You never get up this early."

I looked at her, unsure if I should be happy she knew this about me or worried that she might think me lazy. I opted to be glad she'd noticed. "Nice to know I can still surprise you after all these months. But how are you going to ride in that?" She was wearing another dress, this one a long-sleeved, high-necked blue one with tiny white buttons up the front. The top part was fitted, the skirt billowing out somewhat like an upside-down umbrella. The design made the most of her slender figure and accentuated her curves. I looked away before I could be caught staring.

"This is a riding dress," she said. "But it will be interesting since I've only ridden side saddle a couple of times as a teen at my aunt's medieval reenactments."

"I see." Balancing with both legs on one side of the horse had to be challenging. "And I suppose the hat is to keep the sun off your delicate face."

"Right. I am so losing it the first chance we get." We both laughed.

In the kitchen, the castle staff gave me hot meat that didn't seem like breakfast, but I certainly wasn't going to object. I ate standing up near a stone counter, as did two soldiers, who eyed me with mistrust.

"I hope they aren't following us," I said, turning my back to them.

Jianne's laugh rang out over the busy courtyard. "They were already here, silly."

"Well, if they do follow us, I'm losing them faster than you lose your hat."

The soldiers didn't follow as we went to the stables, where two saddled horses stood waiting. I made a flourishing bow toward Jianne. "After you, my Lady."

Jianne placed her hands on her hips. "You're supposed to help me up."

"Oh, right." I shoved the food package into the convenient saddlebag and reached for her waist, lifting her onto the odd saddle as the stable boy held the reins, feeling relief that I managed to do it. She adjusted her seating, winking at me as if knowing my thoughts.

"At least this is the style I can sit kind of straight on," she said. "It's Sophia's saddle made only for her. Did you know that here in Beaumont, women began to ride like men in the fifteenth century? Not all the time, mind you, but certain women did."

"Unfortunately, we're still in the fourteenth century."

"Late fourteenth century. Close enough. I think I'll bend Sophia's ear about it."

"Right." I nodded in acquiescence. Sometimes I felt we interacted like a married couple. Jianne certainly didn't seem to have any issue with her confidence where I was concerned. Was that a good thing? Or did it mean she'd never look at me as a love interest?

She motioned to the servant. "The reins, please," she said in French.

"I can lead you, m'Lady," the boy protested. "Or I can give them to your brother."

"No need." The tightness in her voice brooked no argument. "I am quite experienced. Give them here." She waved her fingers, and the child obeyed. Jianne awarded him with a smile, and then, with her back straight, she proceeded to lead the way through the peasants in the courtyard to the back entrance. Only then did her posture sag.

"I almost fell off into that pile of horse dung by the back gate," she confessed.

"Really?" I lifted a brow. "You seemed completely in control." I was also having a little difficulty with my own saddle and was grateful my brief jaunt yesterday had given me some experience.

"Stop that," Jianne said, narrowing her eyes at me. "Every time you raise just one brow, I wish I could do it."

I grinned. "Keep trying."

"Right. Well, you can't arch your right one yet, so you haven't really proven it's a trait you can learn."

She looked so striking balancing on that horse in her

voluminous skirt that I had to say, "Maybe not, but I love watching you try." She flushed and looked away, which was also endearing, though I wouldn't dare voice that aloud.

"So where are we going exactly?" I asked.

She looked at me, raising both brows in such a concentrated way that I knew she was trying to arch only one. "To the witch, of course. But we can ride around one side of the wall on the way there and the other on the way back. She lives in a little cottage near a lake."

"The castle lake?" I couldn't remember any ruins there, but the cottage might not have survived the centuries.

"No, it's on the opposite side to the east, closer to Tristan's famed sandwich place. Won't take more than an hour or two on horseback."

"Is it the building where the current restaurant owners live in our time?"

"No, but it's on their property, some distance away from the outer walls of the castle."

"I think I remember seeing the ruins of it, then." We'd started off along the path by the wall before I added, "How did you find her anyway? The witch?"

"Sophia, actually. I told her Mel was sick, and she recommended I get a potion for her. She credits the woman for helping her get pregnant and go full term, so the witch is protected here, whereas elsewhere she might be burned at the stake."

"So we're not in danger of being hung for visiting her?" I asked with a frown. "That takes all the fun right out of it."

She laughed. "Nope, not this time."

"Yeah, but you're not really going to give Mel a potion, are you?"

"Depends on what's in it. You'd be surprised how much

women knew about healing herbs back then. Uh, back here." She shook her head, dislodging the hat that she barely caught on the tip of a finger. "Or whatever."

"Maybe she can tell me what deodorant they use," I said. "How long do they go without baths here anyway?" Before being given my current clothing yesterday, I'd cleaned up from all the digging in a basin I was pretty sure was only for my face, but any deodorizing I'd gained from that was long gone.

"Depends. As the king's cousin, you can order one whenever you want, but the servants might begin to hate you because they have to haul and heat the water. Otherwise, deodorant here is called perfume."

"Great," I muttered.

Her grin lit up her entire face. "Don't despair. Apparently body odor can be very attractive to some."

"If you say so." It might be true for a woman's odor, but my brief stint in the male locker room while playing football in high school had me pretty much detesting the company of all unwashed males.

"Well, this side saddle stuff isn't as bad as I thought," Jianne said, still holding her hat rather awkwardly.

"Oh? Want to race?"

She rolled her eyes in response.

My turn to grin. "Guess that's a no. Here, give me the hat."

She tossed it to me, and I put it on my head, making her laugh again. "Not bad," she said.

"Thank you. It'll keep my complexion nice."

She laughed, so I wore it for another ten minutes before tying it to the saddle bag where it wouldn't be ruined by the horse's sweat.

We took over an hour and a half to clear the outer wall and another twenty minutes to make our way to the witch's residence.

The small stone cottage looked to be dated sometime in the previous century when Castle Forêt had been built. The expansive flowerbeds lining the walkway and circling the structure were meticulously groomed, and herbs sprouted everywhere. At least I assumed they were herbs. We tied the horses to a log that had apparently been set in the ground under a shade tree for this purpose and looked around.

"Good to know a camera won't catch us here, so there will be no evidence that we ever visited," I said.

Jianne laughed. "You mean in case the witch accidentally kills some powerful noble, and the queen has to revoke her protection."

"Well, it is the Middle Ages. You need to listen to your brother, you know."

"Right." She rolled her eyes.

We started up the quaint cobblestone path to the cabin door, but the sound of a person singing brought us around to the back instead, where we found more plants and a black-haired woman of about thirty kneeling in a garden bed with a basket in her hands. Seeing us, she arose and set the basket on a bench under a tree and came to greet us, skirting around hanging bunches of herbs drying on a lower limb.

"Good morrow," Jianne said.

The woman smiled. "Good morrow. What can I do for you?"

"We have a mutual friend," Jianne said. "Someone you helped have a baby."

"Well, that narrows it down to several hundred." The woman's smile widened as a breeze caught the folds of her white dress, which, now that I noticed, looked more like a simple short-sleeved sundress with large pockets that could have been worn in any era. Nothing like the dark, heel-to-wrist material I'd seen the medieval peasant women wearing at the castle. "Who are ye?" she added.

"I'm Lady Jianne Selmone, cousin to the king, and this is

my brother, Emerson." Jianne curtseyed just as she would to any noble woman.

"And now I know the woman you speak of," the witch said. "But please, don't curtsey to me. I am no one of note. Welcome, Lady and Lord." She bowed slightly instead of curtseying. "I'm Viviana Bazin."

Viviana Bazin? Why did that name sound so familiar?

"Very well." Jianne stopped herself in a second mid-curtsey. "We're here, in part, because our sister is expecting and is having trouble keeping food down."

"I can definitely help with some teas and diet changes." Viviana retraced her steps to the bench and picked up her basket, threading it on her arm. "I already have fresh spinach and carrots here, which you can take to her, but I also have some ginger I grow in my greenhouse. It's really the only way to grow it in this climate. Inside the house, there simply isn't enough light. Come."

Greenhouse? I mouthed to Jianne, thinking there was no way they had greenhouses in fourteenth century Beaumont. She shrugged, her expression also curious.

We dodged the drying bunches of plants to follow Viviana toward a stand of trees beyond her garden. "Why is her name so familiar?" I whispered to Jianne.

"Sandwiches," Jianne whispered back without hesitation. "Viviana is the same name as the woman who owns The Chef's Table. Bazin is the family name, so it must get passed down. We do that a lot in Beaumont. Every other generation we have another Jianne in my family. Same with Tristan and Damien's family, and the royal family too, of course."

"Makes sense, I guess."

We emerged from the trees into a clearing where there was indeed a small greenhouse. The frame was stone and wood, but large sections of dense glass spanned the sections of framing.

Viviana opened the door, and a wave of humid heat rolled over us as we peered inside. The glass was bubbly and imperfect, but it let in ample light. Shelves, lattices, and even hanging pots filled every available space. The design wasn't the best from an engineering point-of-view, but it was functional and would extend her production by several months on either side of summer, though without electricity, I doubted anything would grow during the thick of winter.

"But glass is so expensive," Jianne murmured.

"Aye," the woman agreed. "Even glass as hideous as this, but sometimes instead of payment, I ask for favors, and when you give aid to a queen . . ."

"Ah, right."

As we waited near the open door, Viviana ducked under a hanging pot and dropped to a squat halfway through the greenhouse. "I've got a few ginger roots here that are good. Fresh is always better, but I'll have some dried and ready in a few days, which will be more convenient for tea. Just make sure you don't exceed the dosage I'll tell you. I'll also write down a list of foods the cook at the castle should have access to, but if she doesn't, come back here to see me again." She straightened, dodging the hanging plants as she returned to us with several ugly, twisted roots in her hand.

I swatted away a flying insect that had decided to land on my head, probably attracted by my questionable aroma, and stepped outside the greenhouse. "We should probably shut this door so more of these bugs don't get inside."

Viviana sucked in a breath, her head jerking in my direction. "I thought . . . where are you from? Your accent is different. You're definitely not from Beaumont."

"He was raised in Rome," Jianne said quickly. "He spent most of his life there."

Viviana shut the greenhouse door, saying something in a language that was total gibberish to me. I gave Jianne a sideways glance as I said in French, "Excuse me?"

Viviana glared at me. "You were raised in Rome and don't know any Italian?"

"Uh, I was busy studying architecture and engineering."

Viviana snapped her fingers. "American," she said, flushing with excitement. "Your accent is American, and there's only one reason you can be from America when it hasn't been colonized yet. You came through the portal, didn't you? How long have you been here?"

"You know about the portal?" I tried not to gape in astonishment.

"Know about it?" Viviana dropped her root into the basket and brushed dirt from her hand. "I came through it ten years ago and have been stuck here ever since."

Jianne

"No!" I whispered, exchanging a horrified glance with Emerson, thoughts of Mel and her baby and Damien, who had no idea he would soon become a father, swirling in my head.

"Yes," Viviana said firmly, "and if I hadn't been raised at my grandmother's feet and learned about herbs after my parents died, I wouldn't have had any way to support myself. I would have had to work at the castle or marry a poor farmer. A woman can't be here without protection in this era. It's not safe."

"Ten years," I muttered.

"How long for you?" Viviana asked.

"Yesterday," Emerson said. "After lunch. We came through a room inside the stairs near the lake, a room that is only half completed here. We think it might have to be built for us to go back."

Viviana shook her head. "I came through that same little room, and when I got here, there was no room or stairs. Just a weedy lakeside and an annoyed gardener who thought I was stealing his hand rake."

"Hand rake?" I asked.

"Yes. I got stuck inside the room, so I picked up a hand rake from a basket of tools and tried to pry the door open. The next thing I know, I'm tripping backward. Must have hit my head. When I woke up, I was lying in muck next to the lake, and some guy was screaming at me about stealing his rake. I had a huge knot on my head and could barely see. Fortunately, a kind peasant woman took me in. After a few days, I got my bearings and went back, but nothing was there—until they began building last fall before the snow."

"So if it's not the building, what is it?" Emerson asked.

Viviana looked between Emerson and me, her eyes probing. "In the beginning, I followed every lead with any mention of time travel, but I couldn't figure it out. Except . . ."

"Except what?" Jianne and I said together.

Viviana tucked her hair behind her right ear, stepping closer and lowering her voice to say, "Except the witch who owned this cottage before me, the one who the villagers burned right in this very spot, talked about a set of magic tools given to a man who saved a fairy's life. He used them to go back in time and save his wife from some kind of dire fate. I mean, if you believe in such things."

"Which we don't," I began, blood pounding more forcefully through my veins.

"Except we're here," Emerson finished, seeming to know my thoughts.

"Exactly." Viviana stared at us intently. "I searched for the man who found me, but people said he'd moved on."

Emerson glanced at me before saying, "We found tools in the room too. And there was a man who came looking for them right after we appeared here."

Viviana's eyes widened. "Did you touch them?"

"Yes."

"Then maybe you found the rest from the basket I saw. Who was the man?"

"It was a gardener or farmer," I said. "He claimed we stole his tools. He appeared perfectly human. Though now that I think about it, how could his tools have been in that room if it didn't exist in this time yet?"

Viviana shook her head. "I can't say. I never saw him again."

"Something's going on." Emerson looked around as if searching for the answer. "We have to find him."

"When did you leave Beaumont?" I asked Viviana.

She stared at her basket as she thought for a moment. "My memories from there are no longer very clear, which doesn't make sense, but it's like the more I learn and understand here, the more that place seems like a dream. But I remember the twin princes had just turned sixteen or seventeen."

"You mean Gabriel and Jourdain?" I asked. But it had to be them; there hadn't been twin crown princes for a century.

"Yes, those were their names."

"That would make it about ten years," Emerson said. "Their father died, and Gabriel is now king of Beaumont."

"So time is still passing there, just like here." It was logical, of course, but thinking about how worried Damien and Harper and my aunt would be over our absence was heartbreaking.

"Not necessarily," Viviana said. "Because according to the story the witch told, the man who went back had a certain time to fix it and return at the same time to live out his life here with his wife. If he missed the window, he would be missing for years or maybe forever. It was a risk he took. But no one ever knew he left, or so goes the tale. He lived happily into old age with his wife."

Silence fell between us as we contemplated the new concern of a time limit until Viviana cleared her throat delicately. "I'll get this stuff wrapped for you." She turned and began walking back through the trees the way we'd come. "Assuming you really do have an expectant sister," she said over her shoulder.

"We do," I said, keeping pace behind her. "And thank you for the information."

"You're welcome."

As we approached the bench in Viviana's courtyard, I added, "If we find the man and the tools, do you want to come with us? I mean, if it's even possible."

Viviana's step faltered and slowed to a stop. "Once, I would have given anything to go back," she said, turning halfway toward us. "I mean, by the time I left, I had no family to speak of except an uncle who was rather cantankerous, but I missed the modern conveniences and electricity. Now . . ." Her head shifted toward the stone cottage at the sound of a door, where a tall man emerged with two children in his arms, one slightly larger than the other. With him was an older lady who carried a newborn babe. "Now I have more reasons to stay than to leave," Viviana said, looking back at us. "And we have a very good, if simple, life here."

I held her gaze, seeing quiet contentment in her expression. "I'm happy for you."

After a short introduction to her husband, mother-in-law, and three children, Viviana brought us inside the small cottage where more drying herbs hung from bare ceiling beams. She rubbed the ginger root with a damp rag, then wrapped it with several other herbs and vegetables before taking up a small parchment and quill.

"Do you sometimes know what's going to happen?" I asked Viviana as she wrote. "I mean, if you went to school back in modern Beaumont, you had to learn some of the history. Do you find that knowing changes what you do here?"

Viviana's hands paused, her eyes lifting to mine. "Maybe sometimes. For instance, I knew the king and queen wouldn't have a child and that there would be a rather bloody conflict among the royals to determine the new king, so I figured anything I did couldn't make it worse."

"Wait. Did you say you knew they *wouldn't* have a child?" I asked. "Because in our timeline, they did."

Viviana nodded. "Obviously, it changed then. I figured out fast enough that the king was the reason they couldn't conceive and not Sophia. Although they'd bled her with leeches so often, she probably wouldn't have been able to maintain a pregnancy anyway with the lack of nutrition. So I treated them both. Even so, it's a miracle she conceived, and I don't think they'll ever have more." She gave us a sheepish smile. "History came out all right then?"

"Yes, actually," I told her. "No war for the crown at that time, and I'm grateful they have at least the one boy. Sophia will need her son after her husband's gone, and she deserves that. She never does remarry."

"Gone?" Viviana made a sour face. "Maybe I didn't pay as much attention as I thought in school. Wasn't the king murdered because he didn't have an heir?"

"In our timeline, he dies of arsenic poisoning when his son is five. Not here in Forêt, where there will be a second poisoning attempt, but later at the royal palace." I picked up the packaged herbs to occupy my hands.

"A second attempt?" Viviana's brow creased with worry.

Emerson explained about the first poisoning attempt at the capital and the murdered servant. "That's why Sophia insisted on bringing the king here," he said. "But apparently, whoever ordered the poisoning at the palace is here or has someone in place to try again. They won't succeed. Not until later."

"Oh, poor Sophia, to lose him after all that," Viviana murmured. "I have never seen two people more in love. At least not two royal people—and more than a few royal couples have sought me out over the years since I've been under the queen's protection."

Emerson leaned over and put both hands on the table, his face drawn in concentration. "We thought it might be the brother, Constantine, but he becomes regent and later gives up the throne to his nephew when he comes of age."

I gave a little snort. "It could still be him because he contracts some illness and dies. He was too sick to continue ruling and had no choice but to give up control. I read about it last night on my phone. Historians think it was some kind of cancer."

Emerson stared. "And you didn't lead with that this morning? Because if Constantine does something to the king while we're here, we'll be blamed, and we aren't making it back if we're in a dungeon or hanging by our necks."

"Well, I didn't know we could change the past, did I?" I said, giving him a slight glare. "Until now."

He gave me a sheepish smile. "Oh, yeah. Sorry. My bad." His apology was instant, as if he was afraid he'd push me over the edge of some mental cliff. Maybe the comment would have caused anxiety if someone like my father had said it, but from Emerson it didn't feel like criticism but rather an attempt at humor.

Before I could consider that thought further, Viviana spoke. "You say Constantine dies of cancer?"

I nodded. "Is that important?"

"Well, slow poisoning with arsenic is popular in the Middle Ages. It's the poison of the ruling class. Small doses not only eventually kill, but they can also cause cancer and affect fertility, especially when fertility is already compromised. If Constantine dies of cancer, maybe someone targeted both brothers at different times." Viviana whirled and began rifling through a cupboard with jars and vials, settling on one the size of her hand. "I have a detoxifier here that can help in the short term, but really, the key is to find out who's doing it and stop them."

"My bet is back on Constantine," Emerson said, his voice nearly a growl. "He might lose patience in slow poisoning and give the king a larger dose to gain control of the crown. Maybe he poisons others along the way, and the exposure gives him cancer."

"I suppose that could be what happens," Viviana said. "But Sophia really likes him, and she's always been a good judge of character."

The words ignited my guilt. "I don't know about that. She trusts that I'm her husband's cousin."

"And aren't you?" Viviana said. "I may not know my medieval history, but I know who you are, Lady Selmone, and you *are* related to Beaumont's ruling house."

I sighed. "Yes, but not for centuries."

"Irrelevant." Viviana waved my concern away. "Give this to Sophia," she added, pressing the jar into my hand. "Tell her to divide it into ten doses over ten days. It will help him detox at least from small amounts of arsenic, but it can't block anything big. Better to find the source, and fast. Since it happens both here and in the city, it's not the water."

"What are we looking for?" Emerson asked.

"The poison will be in a container or vial with a good lid. Not a pouch. The powder inside will probably be gray, but it could also be white."

She walked us back outside before saying, "Discovering who's doing this might be what you were sent here for."

I blinked at the odd comment. "What do you mean?"

"Well, I've always believed I was sent here to help Beaumont avoid civil war, and also to help Sophia in particular." Her gaze strayed to the children racing each other over the cobblestones. "And for them, of course." She smiled. "But it's your turn now. Fare thee well." She dipped her head and turned from us to join her family.

Emerson was silent as we went around the house to where we'd left the horses. I put the herbs and jar in the saddlebag. "Now what?"

He gave me a slow smile that made my heart skip a beat. "Now we eat. Or you carry me back to the castle lying fainted over my horse. Because something about riding makes me famished."

I laughed. "I thought I heard your stomach growling inside the house. It's probably the protein-rich diet. Your body might be craving carbs, which I've brought. I saw a clearing a short way back where we can eat. Come on!" Now that we didn't have any watching servants, I didn't wait for his help to mount.

"Oh, I see how it is," he said.

I grinned. "I am not a helpless medieval female."

"You ride better than I do, that's for sure. And I doubt there are many helpless females anywhere here or in the future." We laughed together.

The sun felt warm overhead, and I began longing for that ridiculous hat, but I wasn't about to let Emerson know—yet. I could get it after our lunch. We hadn't thought to bring a blanket, but a fallen tree and a large boulder by a stream served as an adequate table and chairs. I unwrapped the bundle of food, featuring cheeses, breads, fruits, and nuts.

We ate for a long moment in silence as I replayed the visit with Viviana in my head. Then I pulled out my phone to check the notes I'd made last night, barely able to see the screen in the bright sunlight. My battery was at ten percent.

"What is it?" Emerson asked.

"Well, I was reading the books last night, and I made some notes here since I didn't have parchment. I actually found a legend that sounds similar to what Viviana was telling us. It's about a fairy who looks like a man. He was in love with a Beaumont princess, and when her life was saved by a gardener, he gave the gardener tools that were supposed to always keep Beaumont safe. It's a legend or maybe a fictional story. You know, like Snow White or Sleeping Beauty."

"Probably," he agreed. Then his grin widened. "But we're still going to find those tools."

He looked so confident sitting there on that fallen log, as if his will alone could make everything all right. A rush of emotion grew so large in my chest that I didn't know how to contain it. Emerson had been nothing but supportive and honorable. Why did I keep pushing him away?

He began making another bread and cheese sandwich. "It makes a lot more sense that it was a human whose life was saved and not a fairy's like in the story Viviana mentioned."

"Stories tend to change over the years," I managed to say, when all I wanted to do was to tell him I was sorry for how I'd been treating him. But I didn't know if the idea came from the submissive part of me that I was trying to excise or the new, confident me that could admit fault without also admitting weakness.

As if alerted by my tone, he looked up from the bread in his hands, his eyes going wide at the sight of my face.

"Emerson," I said, my voice barely a whisper.

"Jianne?"

An obvious question—him asking permission.

I couldn't do it. I couldn't close the space between us.

But he knew me so well that he didn't need me to verbalize my desire. He dropped the bread and reached for me, giving me plenty of time as he had last night. Plenty of time for me to call him friend and push him away.

He *was* my friend, but he was also so much more.

His lips touched mine, slow and steady. Careful. But I wanted more. My arms went around his neck, and he gave a soft groan as I pulled him closer. I could feel the softness of the skin on his neck and the warmth of his hands as he stroked my cheeks and neck. He smelled of outdoors, medieval linen, and, yes, male, but I didn't mind.

I wasn't scared anymore. I finally knew how I felt about him, and I couldn't imagine my life without him. It was just as Mel had said, and what's more, somewhere inside me, I had known it for months now.

Time stopped, and the world around us faded away. I was aware only of him and our lips pressing together. My heartbeat sounded loudly in my ears. Not with panic but with passion . . . and trust. This was a million times better than when I'd kissed him in my dreams.

He drew back, his green eyes picking up even more green from the lush vegetation near the stream. I wanted to tell him not to speak about the future, which might ruin the moment and let my stupid fear rush in.

Thankfully, he simply arched a brow and said, "Wow. Didn't see that coming. Much better than I imagined—and I've got a pretty good imagination." His grin made my stomach flop. "You are worth the wait, Jianne, but I'll warn you now—no matter how long it takes, I'm going to win your heart. Let's make a bet on who will win first. Me winning your heart, or you with arching your eyebrow."

I sputtered a laugh, then he caught my lips once more, and we were soaring into the air and over Beaumont. Maybe I could even see the future.

When we came back to ourselves, I felt giddy and light. "You know we have to go back and check on Mel, right? It's been hours, and we're nowhere near the castle. She needs the ginger."

"*You* have to check on Mel," he corrected. "I'm going to look for some tools."

"We also need to figure out who's trying to kill the king," I said. "Because it's breaking my heart to think of Sophia and her son alone in a few years."

"I may have an idea about that," he said enigmatically.

It wasn't until several hours later, when I was back in the room with Mel and a mug of fresh ginger tea, that I began to worry about what he meant.

Chapter 9

Emerson

I took Jianne back to the castle, flying high from our kisses by the stream. Here, I'd been digging in for the long haul, despairing at how long it might take me to win her heart, and she'd jumped over her own hurdles, bringing me hope and a whole lot closer to my goal. Even if we went backward from this moment, I would know her heart, and it would give me the courage to continue pursuit. Kissing her had only proven that we were more than compatible.

I wanted more of her. I wanted forever.

In fact, the very idea of kissing her again made me feel as if I could leap tall buildings in a single bound.

Or maybe I could find a would-be murderer.

In front of the castle, I gave the reins to a servant and helped Jianne down from the saddle. Her lips looked full and moist, beckoning so strongly I almost forgot that in front of the others, I was supposed to be her brother.

"Say hi to Mel for me," I said with a brightness that was maybe a little too fake.

She narrowed her eyes suspiciously. "What are you going to do?"

"Take the horses back to the barn. And look for some tools."

"Well, be careful."

"Always." I didn't tell her that I was also going to look for the poison, which was another reason I wanted her safely tucked in her suite with Mel. "And you know, that hat is growing on me."

She rolled her eyes and ripped it off her head.

I watched until she disappeared inside, then let the servant take the horses, since that seemed to be what he wanted. Lurking around the castle was not as easy as I thought as I was asked by half a dozen servants if I needed direction to the great hall room, where supper was already about to be served. Our little jaunt had taken far more time than I'd realized. I refused, instead asking questions that eventually led me to the hallway outside Constantine's suite. Hopefully, he'd already be eating in the dining hall, a process I knew from last night could take hours.

I knocked on the door, and when there was no answer, I walked in. "Hello? Constantine? I wanted to ask if you'd heard from the master mason." I felt it was a valid excuse, as they'd had all day to send their fastest rider.

Still, I breathed a sigh of relief when no one answered. I began checking the drawers, closets, pockets of clothing, under the bed, and anywhere else a vial of poison might be hiding. Constantine had far too many clothes and possessions to make it an easy search. I'd nearly finished when a sound at the door had me stepping behind the ugly, heavy curtains hanging on each side of the uncovered window.

Humming came from the person who entered and made a

beeline for the closet. I risked a peek to see Constantine changing his current ridiculous hat for another, even more ridiculous one.

I let out a sigh of relief when he headed to the door without looking in my direction, but my relief disappeared with a knock on the door.

I heard it open. "Hail, Fredrick, what brings you here?"

"Business, Duc Lacort," the steward answered. "Your man is back from seeing the master mason. I cannot find the king, so I am reporting to you."

"The king will not be joining us for supper tonight," Constantine said. "He supped earlier with Sophia and Matis. But I am eager for sustenance, so make haste."

"The master mason will return upon the morrow to recommence construction. He is eager to meet this cousin of yours."

"He approves of the designs?" Constantine sounded weary.

"I think thrilled and amazed would be the more proper terms."

Thrilled and amazed, I thought, unable to stop my grin. And eager to meet me. At least, I think that's what the French words translated to, though I'd have to check with Jianne.

Constantine sighed. "I have to admit, I am myself very impressed with the design, though my cousin, if he is actually a cousin, is quite odd. Sophia will very much enjoy accommodations so close to the lake where she can entertain."

"Your cousins will likely be here for some time," the steward said. "Perhaps you will be seeing more of the lovely Jianne?"

"I intend to do more than see her." Anticipation dripped from Constantine's voice. "I will pursue her ardently. She will make a fine wife."

Over my dead body, I thought, clenching my fists. I'd never wanted to hurl them into someone's face more than I did at that moment.

"I have sent a rider to their castle, however," Constantine added, sounding slightly farther away now. "I need to make sure they are who they say they are. My brother is sometimes too trusting."

"That is very wise," said the steward.

Constantine laughed. "I have to admit that sometimes my brother's naivety is to my advantage."

"You are good to him," the steward protested.

"I do try."

The door closed, and their voices faded.

Had Constantine just hinted at poisoning his brother? Not exactly, maybe, but I hadn't liked his tone. To be honest, I didn't like anything about him.

But I hadn't found poison in any of his rooms.

I waited and listened and finally slipped from the room, grateful that no servants seemed to be in the hall spying on me. I was turned around, though, after my search, and was debating on which way to go when the king rounded a corner with two of the castle guards.

"Hail, Cousin Emerson," he said. "Was your perusal of our walls satisfactory?"

"Indeed, Your Majesty." I gave him a bow. "For the most part."

"Bérenger," he corrected. "We need not stand on ceremonies here. What are your concerns?"

"Some parts of the outer west wall has been removed, I suspect for the expansion of the castle, and it looks like a section of the inner wall is about to be used in the same manner. As you said yesterday, keeping those intact would be wise in case of intrusions from neighboring countries."

I'd butchered every bit of the French conjugations, but Bérenger nodded. "Walk with me."

Okay. We strode through the hallway to a door that led from

the castle out onto the ramparts. Below, I could see the courtyard, less crowded now, as if many of the servants were away for the evening meal. On the other side of the wall, the verdant, rolling hills stretched out as far as I could see. The sun sat low in the sky, and the clear blue sky was so exquisite, my chest almost hurt at the sight. Except for the planted fields and the few peasants still working the land, it didn't look that much different from modern times. It was incredibly peaceful, and I understood why the queen felt safe here.

Further along the parapet, near where the wall angled out toward the lake, Bérenger paused and said, "My brother believes we are wasting time in Forêt. It was he who ordered the stones in the outer wall to be removed. He believes the sooner the expansion and additions are complete, the faster we will return to the palace. We have long had our independence from other nations, and Constantine believes the walls are unnecessary. I indulged him because I understand how difficult country life is for him. And I confess that I too grow weary of hiding here so far from the majority of my people. However, my dear Sophia wants me to remain until we find out who is behind the attempt on my life, and I have difficulty denying her anything."

I considered my words carefully before saying, "I share the queen's concern. Tell me, if you knew there would be an attempt on your life here, would that knowledge bring you closer to discovering the culprit?" I hadn't found poison in Constantine's room, but Bérenger might have his own suspicions about who was involved.

He took a step away, facing me, his hand suddenly on the sword at his side. Some distance away on the wall, the soldiers snapped into readiness. "I'd say that maybe you threaten me, *Cousin* Emerson." Bérenger's emphasis on the would *cousin* was unmistakable.

"No. Not me or my sisters."

He snorted, still alert but calm. "I know you are not Lady Jianne's brother. I see the way you look at her."

I sighed. "Um, is that a problem?"

He barked a laugh. "Nay. Not for me. And if I may speak frankly, under any other noble household, this deception is wise—if you wish to avoid challenge. Noble women are scarce at the moment."

"I'd rather fight than be her brother," I admitted.

"And you'd be run through." Bérenger relaxed his stance, grinning at my expression. "I do recognize my younger self in you. I acted the same way before I won Sophia's heart. You may not know this, but there were a dozen royal princes all over the continent vying for her hand. But pray tell, if you are not after my throne, who is?"

"I think it might be your brother."

Bérenger appeared to consider my words but soon began shaking his head. Sighing, he put his hands on the parapet and stared out over the fields. "What would you say if I told you he saved my life on three different occasions?"

"I don't know. Misdirection?"

He glanced over at me and then back at the fields. "It's not him. Besides, Sophia had him followed. Unbeknownst to me, of course."

"I thought she trusted him."

"With her life, she does, and he loves her too. But she values me over everything except Matis." Pain crossed over Bérenger's face as he stared into the distance. "If he is responsible, my life is not worth living. Aside from Sophia, my brother is my closest friend."

He obviously saw something in the man that I couldn't. "Then who else?" I asked. "How many nobles, spurned lovers, or enemies would be in both places and hate you enough to kill you?"

Bérenger met my gaze. "If another poisoning occurs here, then I might know a way to catch the culprit."

I blinked at him. "You do?"

A half smile quirked one side of his mouth. "Yes. But only if you are telling me the truth."

"I am," I said without hesitation. "I don't know exactly when, but I believe it will occur sometime in the next three weeks." I felt the urge to tell him more, about how he would survive this attempt but not the next, and how his son would reign, Constantine would die childless, and Sophia would never remarry after his death. But the knowledge seemed too cruel.

"Very well," he said, pulling his hand from the parapet. "I will wait until then to send word to Lady Selmone's family, so I can find out who you really are."

"That's fair," I said, having no intention of being around that long.

"Shall we return to the castle?"

"Sure, I—" I'd been about to add that I was hungry when a grizzled peasant came into view below us. Those thin legs in the dirty hose were familiar. "Uh," I said. "If you'll excuse me, I really need to see that man."

Now it was Bérenger's turn to blink. "Do you know him?"

"No, but he has something of ours, or at least something we need. It's very important. A matter of life or death." Which was true given the fact that I wasn't who anyone believed me to be.

"Well, make haste and go after him." Bérenger made a sweeping motion at the peasant, who was retreating through the field.

Frantically, I looked around, searching for a way down from the wall that didn't require going back to the stairs. "But how—"

Before I could finish, Bérenger called to the guards, one of whom sprinted to a turret some distance away and returned with a rope, which he tied around one of the stones on the parapet before disappearing over the side.

I stared down at the very long drop as the man climbed down. This was so much higher than the half-destroyed walls Mel and I had climbed back in the twenty-first century. Bérenger laughed. "Don't tell me you didn't climb your castle walls as a boy. My parents are lucky Constantine and I managed to reach adulthood in one piece. Come on. I'll show you."

He wrapped the rope around his waist and jumped over the edge. Once he safely reached the bottom, I had to follow or lose face altogether. Besides, I needed that peasant. So I went, clinging onto the rope and hoping for the best. Hand over hand I climbed until I finally jumped the rest of the way, my teeth clinking together as I landed.

"With your great ability, you are lucky these walls are so short," Bérenger joked with an irony I could not miss. "Better get after him."

I sprinted across the field, dodging what appeared to be cabbages. At first the peasant didn't notice me and continued walking away, but as I came closer, he heard me and turned to watch my progress with interest.

I came to a stop, heaving beside him. "I need the tools back," I huffed first in English and then in French.

"They are mine," he said in clear French.

"I just need to borrow them. Please. I'll leave them for you by the lake when we're finished." I dragged in a few ragged breaths. "I'll give you whatever you want. Please. My friend is expecting a baby." I made the motions of rocking a baby, though I think I got the words all wrong. It wasn't as if I had gone around talking about babies in French before.

He studied me for a long moment without talking, then he looked past me at the king, who awaited me at the edge of the field. Was the peasant curious to see if the king might intercede? Or was the old man perhaps reading his future? There was no clue on his face to hint at what he was thinking.

Finally, he reached around to a leather bag he carried and retrieved a small spade, which he put in my hand. "You must leave before the sun sets or wait four years." He held up a hand with four fingers.

Four years.

Something gleamed in his eyes, and it told me he knew a lot more about us being there than he was letting on.

"Thank you," I said.

By the position of the sun in the peaceful blue sky, we didn't have much time. Somehow, I had to get the women down to the lake before sunset.

I turned and ran.

Chapter 10

Jianne

"I am glad you told me," Sophia said from the sofa where we sat near Mel's bed. Our patient was still in her nightgown but had finished a light supper and was now thumbing through the books I'd brought from the library.

"You don't think I'm quite mad?" I shifted uneasily, hoping Sophia wouldn't call for the doctor and his container of leeches as the chambermaid had suggested earlier when I'd made several cups of ginger tea for Mel.

She laughed, leaning over to kiss the forehead of her toddler, soundly asleep in her arms. "Not quite. Or rather, I *would* think you mad if I had not known Viviana for so many years."

"She told you?" Mel looked up from the book she was trying to read. We'd been searching for more stories about the fairy or time travel when Sophia had come to the room, and I'd spilled everything.

"Yes, but I confess that I didn't quite believe her until yesterday when I saw you in those strange clothes and speaking with the same accent that Viviana uses." She smiled. "At least you. I'm not sure what language Mel and Emerson speak."

"American English." I sat back, allowing some of the tension to seep from my body.

"And those strange glowing devices you kept peeking at were also a clue, even though you thought I didn't see. And the holes in your ears as well. The church doesn't smile fondly on such things anymore." Sophia sighed. "It's strange to think that my great-grandmother could have holes in her ears for earrings, but on me it would be considered heresy."

"That will swing back again," I said, "though not in your lifetime."

"Unless you change the trend," Mel put in. "You can as queen, you know."

Sophia frowned. "Apparently I won't be queen for long."

My heart ached for her. "But you are forewarned, so maybe you can keep Bérenger safe."

"I can't keep him at Forêt forever. Already he grows anxious to leave."

"Well, I probably broke all sorts of unwritten rules by telling you the future," I said. "But I can't bear the idea of you losing Bérenger if there is anything we can do. You two are perfect together."

"He is my one great love." She straightened the blue blanket around Matis. "Him and our son. And I owe much to Viviana for the time we've had."

"Do you have any idea who might be behind the attempts on your husband's life?" Mel asked.

"Alas, no." She bent to kiss her son's cheek.

"At least now you have more information and can look for someone here who has the poison in their possession." I bit my bottom lip and added, "Do you have someone you can trust to investigate?"

She nodded, her shoulders straightening with determination. "Yes. My family will arrive tomorrow for an extended visit, and with them some lifelong retainers who I trust with my life. And there is also Constantine."

"I'm not sure about him," I said. "He was in both places, after all."

"I trust him," she said firmly.

A sliver of sadness cut into my heart. If Constantine was the culprit, there would be no way to save the king. I glanced at Mel, who gave me a sympathetic smile. We'd done what we could, and at least Bérenger would be safe during their stay here, perhaps even because of the detoxifying herbs we'd brought to Sophia. Maybe that was all we were supposed to accomplish.

I arose to stand before the gilt mirror on the wall. I had changed from my riding outfit to a simple white and teal dress that was less confining than the other finery Sophia had provided, more a stay-at-home dress rather than something for public consumption as befitted my supposed station. Sophia had also insisted on gifting me with a matching set of heirloom jewels of the same color, though I wasn't sure what the stones were, perhaps some aquamarine. She'd even given me the earrings, though I hadn't put them on, knowing the current feeling toward piercings in Beaumont.

But in truth, my perusal was more an excuse to look out the window to see if there was any sign of Emerson. I'd begun worrying about his cryptic comments regarding his ideas to catch the poisoner. Why wasn't he back? Could he be in trouble? I should never have let him wander off alone here.

Mel looked up from the book she was reading. "I think I've found something." She rose from the bed, bringing the book to us.

She had more color in her face now and hadn't run to the chamber pot in more than thirty minutes. "Maybe. I'm not sure."

I took the book from her and sat again next to Sophia, who leaned over to peer at the text. A beautiful illustration in the corner of the page caught my attention.

"Oh, it's one of the books I copied from the library at the palace," Sophia said. "A monk did the illustrations for me."

"Your handwriting is beautiful." Mel gingerly touched the letters as if afraid to smear them.

"Yes, though the flourishes make it hard to read, I know," Sophia said. "But I remember the story well. It's a fairy tale about fairies who take human form to protect Beaumont. They traverse between times, and every now and then, humans are caught up in their schemes. This particular story is about a man who tried to cheat a fairy of his magic. The man, of course, ended up with nothing because the fairy neglected to tell the human how the magic worked—that it had a time constraint."

I sighed as I skimmed the story. "That doesn't really tell us anything, except that we might not—" I broke off, seeing Mel's stricken face.

"What if I can't get back to Damien?" Her hand went to her abdomen where her baby grew unaware and unconcerned.

"We're not giving up."

A banging on the door startled all of us, even waking the child in Sophia's arms.

"It must be the servant I asked to come for Matis," Sophia said. "Though why they would cause such—"

"Jianne, Mel, it's Emerson," he called through the door in English. "We need to leave now."

I jumped up and ran to let him in, with Mel on my heels, as Sophia calmed her child. I'd barely reached for the door when Emerson burst into the room on his own accord.

"Good, you're decent," he said. "I've got one of the tools. At least I hope." He held up a spade. "But we have to be down at the lake by sunset, and since it's early May, that doesn't leave much—" He noticed Sophia and stopped talking.

"You can talk in front of her," Mel said. "We told her everything."

I took his hand. It felt warm and strong but slightly humid from his apparent race here. "You found the man?"

"Yes." He paused. "Or maybe he found me—or let me find him. Anyway, he knows a lot more than he's saying. But if we don't go now, we'll have to wait four years."

"Then let's go!" Mel stepped toward the door.

"But you need to dress!" Sophia called.

Mel looked down at her very ugly but modest shift. "I don't care."

"It won't take but a minute." Sophia gave her waking son to Emerson and hurried to the closet to pull out a gown. Together we helped Mel dress in record time as Emerson played nursemaid in the hall.

"Go, go," Sophia said as we joined him. "I'll be right there. I'm just gathering a few things." To the servant, who had finally appeared to take the young prince, she said, "Please find my husband! Tell him it's urgent."

"We'll have to run," Emerson said as we sprinted to the stairs. "Because waiting for them to saddle the horses might take too long and may not save us any time. Mel, can you do it?"

"Of course. If it means getting back, I can fly there!"

We ran out of the castle and through the courtyard, heading toward the back entrance. Peasants stopped and stared as we ran through the fields.

"It's farther than I remember," I said, puffing. Emerson's hand tightened on mine. "We've still got time."

We reached the top of the lake as the sun dipped partway behind the trees. "Hold up your dresses so you don't trip," Emerson said. Worry came through his voice, and I wondered if maybe we should have waited for the horses. At least the shoes Sophia had given us didn't have heels, though they weren't nearly as practical as Emerson's medieval leather boots.

Mel stumbled, but Emerson grabbed her. "Careful."

"But how do we use the tool?" I asked. "Did he say?"

"No. Let's just get to the room and give it a try."

At last, we reached the bottom of the valley, where a deep trench now cut into the ground in front of the half-built room. "Oh, I forgot about that," Emerson said. "I was looking at the foundation."

"No wonder you were worried about deodorant," I muttered.

"It's a bit far to jump over in these dresses," Mel panted. "Did you really have to dig that long of a trench?"

"I had to check more of the foundation to be sure I wasn't jumping to conclusions." He bent over and held onto the side before jumping into the hole. "Come on. Step on me to get across."

He'd helped Mel into what would be the doorway of the little room when a shout drew our attention. The king and queen were at the top of the valley, heading in our direction on horseback, followed by two soldiers who remained at the top as the royal couple descended.

I glanced at the sun. It had now almost disappeared, and an eerie twilight had taken over the lake. "Hurry," Emerson said. "Come across."

I used his hand as a step to get across the ditch, where Mel steadied me. Her other hand gripped the spade we'd decided she would hold on to, in case that mattered. Her getting back to the future was our primary concern.

I reached down for Emerson. "Come on. I'll help you up."

"I got it." He pulled himself up into the doorway, using the beginning of the stone frame.

Sophia and Bérenger had made it down to us now, and Sophia jumped from her horse without waiting for her husband's help. She hefted a large traveling bag, staggering under its weight. "Here," she said. "I brought this for your castle. You said all the books had been lost, so here are those I have copies of back at the palace. And there are more things to show your aunt. I wish I could meet her."

Bérenger took the bag from his wife and threw it over the ditch. Emerson caught the bag, giving the man a solemn nod.

"Thank you," I called to Sophia.

"Fare thee well," she called back.

"Hurry," Mel urged from behind me.

With a wave at Sophia, I followed Mel through the narrow space, feeling Emerson moving behind me. I could now see the middle of the half-built room and Mel waiting there for us.

I turned to grab Emerson's hand, but the bag Sophia had given him got caught on something, and he was backtracking, searching for a way to release the bag. The room around me seemed to blink and wave. Emerson shifted out of view and then back again.

"Emerson, no!" Because I wasn't going back to our time without him. I would rather stay here in the past than be without the man I loved.

I leapt toward him, grateful when I felt the solidness of his body. Then he was falling, and I couldn't feel him.

Terror struck me—until I landed on top of him. His arms went around me, and I clung tightly to him as his lips found mine.

"I love you," I told him between desperate kisses.

"Good," he said. "Because I am absolutely, completely in love with you too."

"Even if we have to stay here forever," I said, "I would rather do without cell phones and electricity and running water and jeans than be without you."

"Me too." He kissed me again.

Chapter 11

Emerson

*J*ianne's weight pushed my back into the stones, but I didn't care about the discomfort, only that she was kissing me with as much abandon as I was kissing her. A clearing throat made us both look up to see Mel standing over us. I was about to exclaim in dismay that she hadn't made it to the future either when I noticed the ceiling of the room and that her face was lit by a slice of light coming from somewhere.

I tilted my head back on the hard floor to see a doorway beyond my head, one with a half-open door that hadn't existed where we'd just come from. I climbed to my feet, dragging Jianne up with me. "I think we made it!"

"We made it somewhere," Mel said. "Let's get outside. Does anyone have any battery left to go online and see where we are? My phone is completely dead."

"Mine too," Jianne said.

I led them through the narrow hallway to the outside where the sun shone brightly overhead. There was no sign of the trench I'd dug, and the stairway to the lake was complete, with only slight wear and erosion in sight.

Mel stared. "It's not ruined. And look up there. The building Jianne designed is on the landing." She pointed. "They must have used our plans."

I whipped out my phone, but the phone died before I could connect. "Sorry," I said to Mel's eager face. "But look at the sun. It seems to be afternoon here like when we left, not sunset."

"How is that possible?" Jianne asked.

Before anyone could answer, three heads appeared at the top of the valley, soon becoming Harper, Tristan, and Damien. Mel gave a cry and started up the valley toward them. When she reached Damien, she threw herself into his arms and began kissing him urgently.

"Did something happen?" Harper asked, moving past them to join us. "And what is that you're wearing?" Her eyes narrowed. "Is this some kind of a prank?"

I looked down at my tunic, hose, and boots, helpless for an explanation.

"What about the pastries?" Tristan set down a cooler that must contain the drinks they were supposed to bring. "This is a cover-up for eating all the pastries, isn't it?"

"No, *we* didn't eat them all," I said, "and you'll never believe who did. But if you go inside that room and see any garden tools, take my advice and don't touch them."

Damien and Mel were coming toward us now, and I heard him say gently. "Are you okay?"

"No. Yes." Tears began in her eyes. "I mean, I'm pregnant, and I thought I'd never see you again."

"You're pregnant?" Damien whooped and picked Mel up,

whirling her around. "That's amazing! You have made me the happiest man alive!"

Mel laughed until he put her down. She waited until they reached us to say, "It's not exactly the way I wanted to tell you, but when I thought I'd never see you again, I just couldn't wait." Her voice wobbled on the last words, and knowing her as well as I did, I knew she was close to tears.

Damien must have known it too, because he wrapped both arms around her. "What happened?" he asked.

She shook her head and buried her face in his chest. When nothing more was forthcoming, Damien looked at us expectantly. "Why don't you guys try telling me?"

I reached for Jianne's hand, rubbing my thumb across the softness of her skin, an action that didn't go unnoticed by Harper.

"Okay, now I know we've missed something even bigger than a baby," Harper said, grinning widely at us. "Let's go over to the dock and sit down. You can spill everything."

"Wait," Mel said, lifting her head. "Gabriel and Kami are still king and queen of Beaumont, aren't they?"

I held my breath as I waited for the answer. It was possible that our messing around in the past had changed the line of succession and that maybe Mel's sister, Kami, hadn't married Gabriel shortly before he became king.

"Of course they are. Did you hit your head?" Harper asked. "Damien, check her for a fever, would you?"

"I'm fine." Mel pushed his hand away.

"Can I use your phone?" Jianne asked Harper. "My battery's dead."

"Okay, but let's sit down. Mel isn't looking so well."

We made our way to the beautiful dock decorated with fancy stone benches that had certainly not been there before our visit to the past.

"The walls," I said to Harper as we sat. "Pretend we don't remember what we told you this morning about the inner and outer walls. What's their condition?"

Harper blinked at me in surprise but went along with my request. "You said all the inner walls are perfect and only need a few stones replaced and a few repaired, and that the outer wall needs several larger sections replaced because they were cannibalized at the beginning of the castle renovations in the fourteenth century. But you said they've withstood the centuries better than you ever imagined, especially these lake stairs, which show an unusually strong foundation for the time period. The wall repairs are going to fit perfectly in our renovation budget and be completed within the next six months at the same time we finish the castle."

I exchanged glances with Mel. "That's amazing," I murmured. Because I was beginning to remember the conversation almost as clearly as the actual events that had transpired.

"It is," she agreed. "Only six months instead of two years to completion. I can't believe it, and yet . . ."

I laughed. "We designed ourselves right out of two years of job security."

"What are you talking about?" Harper demanded.

For perhaps the first time in my life, I was at a loss for words. How to prove to her where we'd been? Wait, the travel bag I was still carrying might have answers. Opening it, I drew out five handwritten, illustrated books, along with a pair of aquamarine earrings, a gold serving plate, a gold candelabra, and several fancy dresses, including Jianne's gold and red dress that had taken my breath away.

"Did you find these in the little room?" Harper asked, her eyes widening as she examined our haul.

"Not exactly," I said. "Though the books are meant for you and Tristan."

"Wait!" Jianne jumped up from the bench next to me, waving Harper's phone. "I found it! And Bérenger didn't die!"

"No way." I rose and stepped toward her to see what she'd found.

She pointed to tiny words on the screen. "Bérenger Lacort didn't die, and neither did his brother, Constantine." Her excited eyes met mine. "Apparently, they foiled a poisoning attempt at this very castle, carried out by Fredrick, the castle steward, who happened to be the estranged son of a rival family seeking the throne. Killing the king and helping install his family was supposed to be his way back into their fold. Needless to say, the man was hanged for treason."

"And Sophia and Bérenger?" Mel asked.

"Lived happily ever after. They didn't have more children, but they enjoyed many grandchildren and lived into their fifties. That's practically a hundred these days." Her grin widened. "We made a difference."

"*You* made the difference," I said. "You're the one who knew that background and found the witch."

"Witch?" Tristan and Harper asked together.

"Viviana Bezin." I looked at Tristan. "Well, most likely the many great-grandmother of the current Viviana. No wonder those sandwiches taste like magic." I didn't really believe that, but I'd tease him all the same.

"What are you talking about?" Tristan said. "Will you please start at the beginning?"

"Yes, spill it right now," Harper ordered.

Mel, her hand entwined with her husband's, had recovered enough to take the lead, and I was content to let her because I was occupied with Jianne. I put my arm around her waist, and she curled into me, fitting perfectly. Her eyes met mine, and I could see the future there that had been waiting all along.

Soon I'd ask her to marry me. Here, in this very spot and in the same clothes we'd worn in the past and would wear for the ball we were going to throw in six months' time when the renovations were complete.

By then she'd be ready, and I knew she'd say yes.

achel Branton has worked in publishing for over twenty years. She loves writing women's fiction and traveling, and she hopes to write and travel a lot more. As a mother of seven, it's not easy to find time to write, but the semi-ordered chaos gives her a constant source of writing material. She's been known to wear pajamas all day when working on a deadline, and is often distracted enough to burn dinner. (Okay, pretty much 90% of the time.) Under the name Rachel Branton, she writes romance, romantic suspense, and women's fiction. Rachel also writes urban fantasy, paranormal romance, and science fiction under the name Teyla Branton. For more information or to sign up to hear about new releases, please visit www.RachelBranton.com.

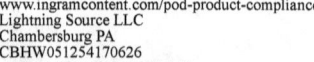